THE FABLED FIFTH GRADERS OF AESOP ELEMENTARY SCHOOL

THE FABLED FIFTH GRADERS OF AESOP ELEMENTARY SCHOOL

Candace Fleming

schwartz & wade books · new york

For the endlessly energetic Patty Williams and her talented WSIC Tech Team at Washington Elementary School—thanks for the inspiration!

Copyright © 2010 Candace Fleming

All rights reserved. Published in the United States by Schwartz & Wade Books, an imprint of Random House Children's Books, a division of Random House, Inc., New York.

Schwartz & Wade Books and the colophon are trademarks of Random House, Inc.

"Ah! Sweet Mystery of Life," words and music by Rida Johnson Young and Victor Herbert, recorded by Nelson Eddy and Jeanette MacDonald in the 1935 movie *Naughty Marietta*. "O, my luve's like a red, red rose," by Robert Burns, 1759–1796.

Visit us on the Web! www.randomhouse.com/kids

Educators and librarians, for a variety of teaching tools, visit us at www.randomhouse.com/teachers

Library of Congress Cataloging-in-Publication Data
Fleming, Candace.
The fabled fifth graders of Aesop Elementary School / Candace Fleming. — 1st ed.
p. cm.
Summary: Throughout their fifth-grade year, a group of rambunctious students learn fable-like lessons from extraordinary activities, singing guinea pigs, and eccentric teachers, led by the inimitable Mr. Jupiter.
ISBN 978-0-375-86334-9 (hc) — ISBN 978-0-375-96334-6 (lib. bdg.) — ISBN 978-0-375-89497-8 (e-book)
[1. Schools—Fiction. 2. Teachers—Fiction. 3. Behavior—Fiction.] I. Title.
PZ7.F59936 Fac 2010
[Fic]—dc22
2009031052

The text of this book is set in Nimrod and Congress Sans.
Book design by Rachael Cole

Printed in the United States of America
10 9 8 7 6 5 4 3 2 1

First Edition

Random House Children's Books supports the First Amendment and celebrates the right to read.

CONTENTS

IN A CLASS OF THEIR OWN

ON THE FIRST DAY OF SCHOOL, Mr. Harry Valentine Jupiter—Aesop Elementary's only fifth-grade teacher—rose early. After brewing himself a cup of rose hip tea (harvested during his recent trek through the Andes Mountains), he sat down at his Tang dynasty writing table to review his class list.

Yes, they were all there—every single one of his students from last year.

These were the kids other teachers called "rambunctious," "high-energy," and even "naughty." No one dared teach them.

"Not for love or money," their former first-grade teacher, Ms. Bucky, had said. Her time with the children had left her with a tooth-grinding problem.

"Not for all the tea in China," their former second-grade teacher, Mrs. Chen, had added. The muscles in her chin *still* twitched from the experience.

"Ye gods, no!" their former third-grade teacher, Mr. Frost, had yelped. "Another year with them and I won't have *any* hair left!"

Only one teacher had been willing to take on these kids—Mr. Jupiter. He had journeyed with them through fourth grade. Now he looked ahead to fifth.

"It will be as thrilling as bungee jumping off the Empire State Building," he told himself, "as challenging as discovering the lost city of Atlantis; as rewarding as catching (and releasing) the Loch Ness monster."

Plucking a green feather from his Aztec headdress, he used his obsidian ceremonial blade to cut the feather's tip into a pen point. Dipping the quill into his bottle of ox-gall ink, he opened his parchment grade book and wrote each student's name with a flourish.

He paused a moment, sipping his tea and thinking. Then beside each name he added a few personal notes.

Ashlee Anderson—Possesses the optimistic, encouraging heart of a cheerleader; is fond of unicorns.

Stanford Binet—Always prepared—always! Never ceases to amaze me with the depth and breadth of his knowledge, which can make him a tad bit superior at times.

Bernadette Braggadoccio—Her bold, brash, and blustering exterior conceals, I believe, a highly inquisitive mind. Just ask her!

Ashleigh Brown—Ditto on the heart of a cheerleader and unicorn collecting. Why haven't I noticed this similarity before? Hmmm . . .

Rose Clutterdorf—Always a ray of sunshine in the classroom, despite her best efforts; and she always manages to smear and wrinkle whatever she comes in contact with.

Lillian "Lil" Ditty—A poetic little soul, she hears the music in words; will burst into verse whenever the muse calls—in the middle of math, during a spelling test . . .

Emberly Everclass—Disciplined, and until last year's bout with chicken pox, had never missed a day of school; an analytical thinker, he loves reading, especially mysteries.

Jackie Jumpbaugh—This girl plays a mean game of tetherball, and kickball, and basketball, and floor hockey, and . . . you name it, she excels at it.

Melvin Moody—What to do about meek, overlooked Melvin? His classmates ignore him, but

I believe he has hidden talents; will he expose them this year? I'll keep my fingers crossed.

Ernest Moomaday—Rembrandt with crochet needles, he has a real gift with yarn; in a week this boy could cover a football field with a perfectly crocheted inverted-V-stitch cozy.

Humphrey Parrot—Observant; a true mimic, perhaps his way of thinking things through, or . . . is it something else? Have Nurse Betadine check his hearing.

Rachel Piffle—Shy, painfully shy, but you can see the intelligence in her eyes. Will she find her voice this year?

Missy Place—Clever, but absentminded; loses everything . . . anything: mittens, textbooks, backpack, lunch box (we've yet to find that lunch box).

Hamilton "Ham" Samitch—Has the appetite of a Saint Bernard—no doughnut is safe.

Victoria Sovaine—Can be somewhat self-involved; has yet to discover her true inner beauty, but I have hopes.

Amisha Spelwadi—Quick-minded and competitive;

school legend has it that she spelled the word
a-m-b-i-d-e-x-t-r-o-u-s in her sleep during kindergarten naptime.

Calvin Tallywong—Strangely fond of the taste
of cedar—as in wooden pencils; bright but
mathematically challenged.

Bruce Vanderbanter—One half of the comedy
team of Vanderbanter and Wittier; tossed out some
of the best one-liners I've heard since I toured the
Mongolian vaudeville circuit. I must work harder
not to laugh at his jokes.

Leonard "Lenny" Wittier—The other half of the
above-mentioned comedy team; a quick, nimble
mind—without a lick of discipline.

Ashley Zamboni—I am told he can burp the
alphabet, although I've not yet had the pleasure; a
bit sensitive about his name, and with the middle
name of Valentine, I understand.

Mr. Jupiter put down his quill and reread his
notes. "Yes, they can be trouble," he said to himself,
"but . . ." He grinned. "I wouldn't have *my* class any
other way."

Drying the ink with his blotter, he closed his grade book and put on his headdress.

Time to go to school.

MORAL: One man's pain may be another man's pleasure.

A BRAND-NEW SCHOOL YEAR

A FEW HOURS LATER, AESOP Elementary School's faculty gathered in the teachers' lounge for their annual Kicking-and-Screaming-into-the-New-Year breakfast.

"Yummy, yummy in my tummy," chirped Miss Fairchild, the kindergarten teacher, as she popped a melon ball into her mouth. "Mmm-mmm-good."

"Food, glorious food," sang the music teacher, Mr. Halfnote, as he spread cream cheese on a blueberry bagel. "May I have some more?"

"Chocolate," grunted the gym teacher, Mrs. Gluteal, as she bit into a brownie. "Need chocolate."

Mrs. Struggles, the school's principal, strode into the lounge. "Twenty minutes until the bell rings," she reminded them in her brisk manner. Then, pointing out the window, she added, "And look, our students are already arriving—bright-eyed and eager for another year of learning."

The teachers looked.

Outside on the blacktop, chaos reigned.

Kindergartners picked their noses and shrieked, "Mommy!" First graders drooped and staggered beneath the weight of their school supplies. Second graders raced back and forth, snatching away hats and exposing fresh buzz cuts. Third graders smacked and pounded each other with their new backpacks, while fourth graders rolled their eyes at the younger kids and tried to look cool. All the while, parents—thrilled that summer vacation had finally come to an end—milled about, snapping pictures and beaming from ear to ear now that all was right with the world.

The sight made Mrs. Gluteal yelp, "Brownies! Where are those brownies?" She pushed her way to the table, only to discover that the serving trays were half empty. "We're going to need more food," she declared.

In a flash, the teachers shook out their lunch bags and cleared out their fridge. They fortified themselves with a cornucopia of cuisine—powdered doughnuts, chips and salsa, spinach quiche, leftover artichoke dip, low-fat frozen dinners, turkey chili, baked potato chips, salami and cheese, microwave pizza, raspberry truffles, party mix, chocolate kisses, pumpkin scones, and celery sticks (although no one touched those).

"Eat up," advised Mr. Frost, the third-grade teacher. "We're going to need every ounce of strength we can muster."

For several minutes the only sound in the lounge was chewing.

Then Mrs. Chen, the second-grade teacher, dabbed a speck of tuna salad off her chin. "Things could be worse," she said. "We could be teaching *fifth grade.*"

The chewing ceased.

"Oh, my, yes . . . the fifth graders . . . oh, dear . . ."

Mrs. Fairchild let out a little sob.

Mr. Frost broke out in a cold sweat.

Mrs. Gluteal lost her appetite.

Fifth graders!

The very words struck fear into the teachers' hearts.

Only Miss Paige Turner, the school librarian, remained unruffled. Taking a sip of her rose hip tea, she said, "Luckily, the fifth graders have the perfect teacher."

"Hmph!" snorted Bertha Bunz, the lunchroom monitor. "Perfectly *weird,* you mean."

"Now, now," cautioned Mrs. Struggles. "Let's not gossip about our colleagues, especially those who aren't in the room."

"Who's gossiping?" replied Mrs. Bunz. "I'm just stating a fact. And the fact is Mr. Jupiter is weird—and his students are following in his weird footsteps."

Mrs. Playwright, the drama teacher, nodded in agreement. "I heard that Mr. Jupiter spent his summer spelunking in Zanzibar."

"Spelunking?" said the janitor, Mr. Swill. "Who spends their summer in a cave?"

"Weird!" everyone agreed—everyone, that is, except Miss Turner. She took another sip of tea and didn't say a word.

"I read in the newspaper that he discovered a new species of blind cave slug," added Mrs. Shorthand, the school's secretary.

"Weird," the others repeated.

Miss Turner took another sip of her tea and still didn't say a word.

"He told me he designed and built his own biplane, then flew it across Africa to Zanzibar," said Mr. Halfnote.

"And he flew solo except for a parrot he claims he

brought along because of its impeccable sense of direction," added Nurse Betadine.

"Weird."

"Just like his students," declared Mrs. Bunz. "They deserve each other."

At that precise moment a spectacular feathered headdress shaped like a toucan passed by the open window. Its orange and green plumage rustled in the morning breeze, and its hooked golden bill glinted in the sunlight. "Good morning, all," called the toucan.

The teachers gaped.

"Is that Mr. Jupiter?" asked Mrs. Shorthand.

"Wearing an Aztec headdress?" asked Mr. Swill.

Mr. Jupiter waved to his fellow educators. Then he called over his shoulder, "Come along, class."

Behind him, marching one by one like a line of baby ducklings, came the brand-new fifth graders. Each wore a headdress identical to Mr. Jupiter's.

"Does this headdress clash with my outfit?" asked Victoria Sovaine.

"I don't know about you, but I look like an Aztec princess," replied Bernadette Braggadocio.

"I hope I don't lose mine," fretted Missy Place. "It's still on my head, right?"

"Pffft," said Rachel Piffle shyly.

"I think a crocheted ceremonial robe would really complete this outfit," said Ernest Moomaday.

"Get serious," snorted Stanford Binet. "Aztecs didn't wear yarn. They wore gold and feathers."

"Why do you always have to be such a Mr. Know-It-All-Smarty-Pants?" piped up Emberly Everclass. "Your attitude is a real mystery to me."

"Yeah, a real mystery," repeated Humphrey Parrot.

"You know, I might wear this headdress instead of my football helmet," said Jackie Jumpbaugh.

"The fighting Toucans of Aesop Elementary," cheered Melvin Moody.

Jackie ignored him.

Amisha Spelwadi tapped Rose Clutterdorf on the shoulder. "Don't look now, but you've already managed to get peanut butter on your *h-e-a-d-d-r-e-s-s.*"

"My what?" said Rose.

"Your *h-e-a-d-d-r-e-s-s,*" repeated Amisha.

"Don't spell it, say it," said Rose.

"Your headdress," said Amisha, who was already practicing for this year's district-wide spelling bee. "You've got peanut *b-u-t-t-e-r* on your headdress."

"Peanut butter?" piped up Ham Samitch. "Mmmm, peanut butter!"

Lil Ditty burst into verse:

> *"Aesop Toucans on the first day of*
> *school.*
> *How exciting!*
> *How way cool!*
> *Ain't no dummies.*
> *Ain't no fools.*
> *Readin', writin', and 'rithmetic rules!"*

"You mean math," corrected Stanford Binet.

"Math?" Calvin Tallywong grumbled. "I hate math."

At his words, Ashlee Anderson shook her head, causing her dangly unicorn earrings to dance. "Calvin," she scolded, "you know hating is not allowed in fifth grade."

Ashleigh Brown shook her unicorn earrings too. "That's right," she agreed.

"Don't you just hate that?" joked Ashley Zamboni.

"Hey, Ashley Z.'s being a wise guy," snickered Lenny Wittier.

"It beats being a wise *girl*," giggled Bruce Vanderbanter.

"I'm a boy, and don't you forget it!" shouted Ashley Z.

"Oooh, we're scared!" Lenny and Bruce cried in unison.

At the front of the line, Mr. Jupiter clapped his hands. "Research has shown that Aztec priests and princesses never bickered. Now stop squawking and start dancing."

Crowing with delight, twenty toucans flocked around their teacher.

Pretending they had pom-poms, Ashlee A. and Ashleigh B. thrust their arms into V shapes, then jumped, kicked, and put their fists on their hips. "RAH!"

Rose Clutterdorf did a sloppy slide glide while her best friend, Missy Place, tried to do a moonwalk, but . . . "I've lost the beat!"

Mr. Jupiter clapped his hands again. "Let's see those bird moves!" he cried.

The students flap-flapped their arms. They shook-shook their tail feathers. Then they strut-strut-strutted straight into the school.

In the teachers' lounge, the staff stood open-mouthed.

Then Mrs. Bunz snorted again. "Am I right, or am I right?"

Miss Turner put down her teacup. "Bertha," she said with a smile. "You *are* right. Mr. Jupiter and his students absolutely, positively deserve each other."

MORAL: Birds of a feather flock together.

CLASS CURRICULUM

AFTER STOWING THEIR HEADDRESSES in their hall lockers, the fifth graders headed into their new classroom. It looked exactly the same as last year's. In one corner stood the same old suit of armor and the four Lugunga pig masks. There were the same old ceremonial slit drums and totem pole; the same old shrunken head collection and coelacanth tank, astrolabe and Egyptian sarcophagus. Even Mrs. Yorick's skull was sitting in the same old place on the corner of Mr. Jupiter's desk.

Still, something *was* different. Last year they had been fourth graders, not quite top dogs but no longer school babies. But now . . . now they were *fifth graders.*

"And we're going to ruuuule the schoooool," drawled Lenny. He high-fived Bruce, who hip-bumped Emberly, who thumb-wrestled Calvin, who belly-bashed Ham, who butt-thumped Humphrey, who tried to back-slap Stanford, who sidestepped Humphrey and snorted, "Get serious."

Stanford pushed Humphrey away. He sat down at his desk and looked at Mr. Jupiter. "What are we going to learn this year?"

"I'm glad you asked, Stanford," replied Mr. Jupiter. As the others took their seats, he opened his parchment grade book.

"This is going to be good!" squealed Ernest. He rubbed his hands together. "I can't wait to hear about all the fun we're going to have."

Mr. Jupiter cleared his throat and began to read from his book. "'Students will strategically deploy new vocabulary words for use in spelling, reading, and writing.'"

Rose turned to Amisha. "What's that mean?"

Amisha shrugged. "I'm *b-e-w-i-l-d-e-r-e-d*."

"'Students will explore number patterns, algebra, and geometry and demonstrate evidence of reasoning using said numbers within said systems.'"

"Is that math?" gasped Calvin. "I think he's talking math." He reached for a brand-new number two pencil, jammed the eraser end into his mouth, and began chewing. (Whenever he was nervous, Calvin chewed, and math made him very nervous.)

"'We will also study pre- and postcolonial development of democratic ideals and institutions, including voting and elections.'"

"Everyone who thinks this is boring, raise your hand," said Bernadette.

"'And engage in a concentrated investigative study of the formative and causative years in history,'" continued Mr. Jupiter.

"I think our best school days are past," sniffed Victoria.

Mr. Jupiter closed the book. "Doesn't that sound exciting, boys and girls? And that's just the lesson plan for *this* week."

Lenny and Bruce gagged.

Bernadette groaned.

Rachel drooled in her sleep.

Then Mr. Jupiter tossed the book onto his desk—
FLUMPF!

The sound caused the classroom map of "Mastodon Migratory Routes of the Wurm Glaciation" to roll up with a loud *SNAP!*

Rachel woke with a start. "Pffft," she complained. She wiped the drool off her chin.

"Look!" cried Ashley Z.

There on the blackboard, written in Mr. Jupiter's hand, was a long list. It read:

Some *Other* Things We May Study This Year

- The multiple uses of edible red-green algae

- The six most effective ways to search for extraterrestrial life

- The proper care and feeding of Burmese spectacled guinea pigs

- The seventeen habits of highly defective headhunters

- The life cycle of Bigfoot

- The biography of Marvin Dewey, Melvil's little brother

- The best recipes using salami and butterscotch pudding

- The secret language of the armadillo

- The rain rituals of the Ub-pa-kuyu tribe of the Tatiano Republic

- The seven ways to catch a blind cave slug

"Oh, dear, you weren't supposed to see *that* list," said a smiling Mr. Jupiter. "After all, the curriculum comes first, and these are just a few *supplemental* lessons I'm considering."

Calvin took the pencil out of his mouth. "What's a blind cave slug?" he asked.

Mr. Jupiter pulled a terrarium out from under his desk and set it on top. "I'm glad you asked, Calvin. . . ."

School had begun.

MORAL: Expect the unexpected.

CAT LADIES AND HEAD LICE

MISS TURNER WAS BURSTING WITH excitement. "Fifth graders!" she cried when they arrived in the library with Mr. Jupiter for their very first visit of the school year. "I have thrilling news!"

"You're getting married!" whooped Missy.

Miss Turner's cheeks turned the same shade as her lipstick—Glamazon Jungle Red. "N-no, no," stammered the librarian. "Whatever gave you that idea?"

Missy shrugged. "I don't know. I guess because last Saturday I saw you and Mr. Jupiter coming out of the Aphrodite Cafe together and you were—"

"Ahem." Mr. Jupiter loudly cleared his throat, putting an end to Missy's story.

"I bet I can guess your news!" exclaimed Ernest. "You've won an all-expense-paid trip to the International Library Association's annual conference. Where is it this year, Death Valley?"

"A library conference?" repeated Humphrey. "What's so thrilling about a library conference?"

"Oooh, oooh, I know!" cried Lenny. "They've

discovered that Melvil Dewey's alive and well and living in Las Vegas."

Miss Turner shook her head. "Those are all interesting guesses," she said, "but the truth is so much more exciting." She strode across the library, flung open the storage room door, and . . .

"TA-DA!" she cried.

The room had been transformed. Gone were the mops, buckets, and stacks of paper towels. Now the place hummed with electronic equipment—cameras, microphones, lighting rigs, video monitors—even a teleprompter. Above a small stage hung a sign. It read: WUSS.

"Isn't it wonderful?" said Miss Turner, spreading her arms wide. "The school district purchased a secondhand television station at an anchorman's garage sale last summer, and happily, they've given it to Aesop Elementary."

The fifth graders wandered into the room.

"Who are you calling a wuss?" asked Ham.

"A what?" said Miss Turner.

"A wuss," Ham said again. He pointed to the sign.

"Oh, no," replied the librarian, "those are our call letters. The *USS* stands for the United School System. Fun, yes?"

Ham nodded.

"And here's the truly thrilling part," she continued, her excitement rising. "I have decided to form a fifth-grade media club. Together we will produce a weekly news program that will be broadcast each Monday into every classroom in the school."

"Every classroom?" repeated Humphrey.

Miss Turner nodded.

"We'll be stars!" exclaimed Victoria. "Or at least, *I* will." She batted her eyelashes, gave her hair a flip, and practiced her red-carpet walk. "No autographs, please," she purred.

Lenny let out a scream. "Victoria, wh . . . wh . . . what's that enormous thing on your shoulders?"

Victoria's eyes grew wide. "What? Help! What is it?"

"Oh," snickered Lenny, "it's just your swollen head." He high-fived Bruce.

Victoria flipped her hair again. "Who cares what you say? I'm going to look simply divine on camera." Then she smiled and, in a voice dripping with sweetness, added, "Has anyone ever told you that you have the perfect face for radio?"

"Gee, thanks, Victoria," said Lenny. "That's about the nicest thing you've ever . . . Hey, wait a minute!"

"Yes, well, not all of us can be in front of the camera," Miss Turner said. "After all, there are lots of important behind-the-scenes jobs that need to be done."

"Like what?" asked Ernest.

Miss Turner smiled. "Like wardrobe director, for one," she said. "Someone has to make sure our anchor-girls and -boys look good on camera."

"That's the job of me," said Ernest. "I'll crochet everyone matching vests."

"Wonderful," said Miss Turner. She wrote Ernest's name and job title on a piece of paper.

Rose raised her hand. "Can Missy and I write the news?" she asked.

"In television it's called copy, and you certainly can," said Miss Turner. She added their names to her list.

Amisha raised her hand. "Can I double-check their copy to make sure everything's spelled right?"

Miss Turner nodded. "That makes you the copy editor. But you'll have to check facts as well."

Amisha grinned. "Copy editor. It has a nice *r-i-n-g* to it, doesn't it?"

Now Calvin spoke up. "I want to be the cameraman."

"That's a difficult job," said Miss Turner. "You'll

need people to help you with lighting and sound. Does anyone want to join the crew?"

Humphrey, Emberly, and Ashley Z. raised their hands.

Miss Turner wrote all their names down.

"Ashleigh B. and I can make scenery," volunteered Ashlee A.

"Pffft," added Rachel.

Miss Turner didn't hear her.

"Designing a set is lots of work," said Miss Turner. "Would anyone else like to help?"

"Pffft," Rachel said.

Miss Turner looked around the room. "Anyone?"

"Pffft," Rachel said again.

"Then I'm going to have to volunteer people," said Miss Turner. She scanned her class list. "Let's see, Lil Ditty and . . ."

"Pffft!" Rachel said frantically. "Pffft! Pffft!"

"Rachel Piffle," concluded Miss Turner.

"Pffft," Rachel said with a smile.

Miss Turner tapped her paper with her pencil. "All the behind-the-camera jobs have been filled. That leaves only anchor positions. Volunteers?"

Lenny's hand shot into the air. "Can Bruce and I tell a weekly joke? We'll be the school comedians."

"The class clowns," agreed Bruce. He turned to Lenny. "Tell me again. Why won't cannibals eat clowns?"

"They taste funny," answered Lenny.

The boys howled with laughter.

"Get serious," snorted Stanford. "Our news program can't be all fun and games. I think we should have a segment on current events."

"*I* want to do a health and beauty spot," said Victoria.

"And I want to be the sports announcer," said Jackie.

Miss Turner nodded. "I think those are all wonderful suggestions."

"Can I announce the week's menus?" begged Ham. "Can I? Huh?"

"Of course," said Miss Turner.

"And can I read the week's announcements?" asked Melvin.

The others ignored him.

"Who's going to read the week's announcements?" asked Calvin.

Miss Turner scanned her class list. "There are

only two people still without jobs—Bernadette and Melvin."

"I don't want to read any silly announcements," said Bernadette.

Miss Turner looked up from her list. "What *do* you want to do?" she asked.

Bernadette thought a moment. "Exposés," she finally said. "Piercing, probing investigative reporting. I will ferret out the answers to our viewers' most burning questions. What *really* is in Cook's mystery casserole? What *really* goes on in the teachers' lounge? What were you *really* doing with Mr. Jupiter last Saturday night?"

"Ahem." Mr. Jupiter cleared his throat again.

"Strike that last question," said Bernadette.

"What do you know about investigative reporting?" asked Miss Turner.

Bernadette shrugged. "What's to know? You investigate, and then you report. Easy peasy."

Miss Turner fell silent, considering. Finally she said, "All right, Bernadette. I'll give you a chance. You are now a WUSS investigative reporter."

"Does that mean I get to read the announcements?" asked Melvin.

* * *

Two weeks later, the fifth graders went on the air.

Melvin straightened his crocheted vest (blue worsted wool using the half-double stitch), cleared his throat, and looked into the camera.

"In three . . . two . . . ," whispered Calvin and raised his finger, ". . . one."

The camera's green On light blinked on.

"I'm Melvin Moody and you are watching WUSS."

Lenny and Bruce snickered.

"And here are your week's announcements." Melvin shuffled through a handful of index cards and read the first one: "Mrs. Bunz is offering a reward for information leading to the return of her megaphone."

He read the second card: "Mr. Halfnote is now holding tryouts for the Aesop Elementary Harmonica, Washboard, and Armpit Band. Anyone interested should meet in the music room after school today. Harmonicas and washboards will be provided. Bring your own armpits."

He read the last card: "Nurse Betadine would like to remind all first graders that boogers are not one of the four basic food groups. Use a tissue."

He laid the cards on the desk. "And now over to Ham Samitch for a look at this week's menu."

Calvin angled the camera to the right.

"*Bon appétit,* lunch lovers," said Ham with a big smile. "It's going to be a dee-licious week here at Aesop Elementary. Monday's entrée is a delightful tofurky surprise, followed by tasty meat nuggets *al forno* (that means baked) on Tuesday; a traditional favorite, yak and cheese, on Wednesday; and on Thursday, an inspired selection of various bratwursts and wieners. On Friday Cook gives us a real treat by serving her famous three-bean sandwich accompanied by lime Jell-O embedded with baloney slices. Mmm-mmm, good!"

The camera moved to Jackie. "In football last night the Bears mauled the Rams, the Lions roared ahead to beat the Chiefs, the Vikings sacked the Cowboys, and the Ravens lost to the lowly Dolphins. After the game, the Ravens' coach quit, saying, 'Nevermore!'"

The camera zoomed in on Stanford.

"In more serious news," droned Stanford, "scientists have discovered the genome that may unravel the mystery of why zebras have stripes and leopards have spots and not the other way around."

"But can scientists unravel the secret of beautiful hair?" interrupted Victoria. "I can. Here's beauty tip number one for all you wanna-be-mes out there. Beautiful hair begins with—"

"Lemon juice and kitty litter," said Lenny.

"That explains why she's such a sourpuss," added Bruce.

The boys grinned into the camera. "And that's your joke of the day," they giggled together.

Victoria's manicured hand could just be seen smacking the back of Lenny's head as the camera angled back to Melvin.

He cleared his throat again. "And now, a hard-hitting report from investigative reporter Bernadette Braggadocio."

The camera panned again.

"Thank you, uh . . . uh . . ."

"Melvin," whispered Melvin.

Bernadette ignored him.

Instead, she pulled out a pair of horn-rimmed glasses, perched them on the end of her nose, and looked deep into the camera. "Students of Aesop Elementary," she said in a very serious voice. "This reporter has uncovered evidence that Cook does not use real cheese in her yak and cheese recipe. Yes, the yak is real. But what is that yellow stuff you've been eating?" Bernadette paused for effect, then declared, "It is processed cheese food, aka fake cheese. And fake cheese just doesn't cut it." She paused again. "This reporter, for one, is shocked. Aren't you?"

The red Off light on top of the camera blinked on.

And Ham hurried over to Bernadette. "Is that true?" he asked. "Is it really fake cheese?"

"Well," said Bernadette, "I heard it from a kid whose brother knows another kid whose mom used to work in the school lunchroom."

"Isn't that called a rumor?" asked Ham.

"They're called sources," corrected Bernadette. "But I wouldn't expect you to understand."

For the rest of the week, Bernadette kept her eyes and ears open for more scoops and sources, but she didn't uncover anything hard-hitting until—

"Have any of you seen the crazy new art teacher yet?" Missy asked during Friday free time.

"Crazy new art teacher?" said Bernadette. She flipped open her black spiral notebook—the one she'd been carrying ever since she'd become an investigative reporter. "Tell me more."

"Her name's Ms. Bozzetto, and she just moved into that creepy old Victorian over on Vesta Street," said Missy. "At least, that's what my neighbor told me."

"She carries around dozens of cat pictures in her purse," said Jackie. "At least, that's what I overheard a fourth grader say."

"And she purrs and mews to herself," said Ashlee A. "At least, I bet she does."

"Her clothes are covered with cat hair," added Victoria with a shudder. "I saw that for myself."

Humphrey leaned into their conversation. "Cat hair? That's because Ms. Bozzetto has hundreds of cats living in her house."

"How would you know?" asked Victoria.

"I heard it from a first grader, who heard it from his babysitter, who heard it from her boyfriend, who heard it from his baseball coach, who probably heard it from his wife, who heard it from their first grader," explained Humphrey.

"Oh," said the girls. They nodded their understanding.

And Bernadette wrote furiously in her notebook, her pencil trying to keep pace with the hard-hitting investigative report that was forming in her mind. Within minutes she had it all down on paper:

Students of Aesop Elementary, I have uncovered evidence that a crazy woman works in our school. Her name is Ms. Bozzetto, and she is our new art teacher. What sent her over the edge? Was it a broken heart? A lifetime's exposure to tempera paints? We may never know.

What we do know is that Ms. Bozzetto has become a crazy cat lady, living in her lonely Victorian mansion with a reported five hundred cats. This explains her hairy clothes, her walletful of kitty portraits, and her tendency to mew instead of saying hello. This reporter, for one, is shocked. Aren't you?

Bernadette put down her pencil and grinned. It was the best investigative report ever!

ZZZZ-CRACK!

The loudspeaker buzzed and crackled. Then the voice of Mrs. Shorthand—who had been an air traffic controller before becoming the school's secretary— filled the room. "Mr. Jupiter? Come in, Mr. Jupiter."

"I read you loud and clear. Go ahead," Mr. Jupiter replied.

"Please send Bernadette Braggadocio to the office," said Mrs. Shorthand. "Do you roger that?"

"I roger that," replied Mr. Jupiter. "Bernadette is on her way."

ZZZZ-CRACK!

The loudspeaker buzzed and crackled off.

Bernadette frowned. "I wonder what they want me for?" she asked.

Mr. Jupiter pointed to the door. "I suggest you go and find out."

Picking up her notebook, Bernadette headed to the office.

When she arrived, Mrs. Shorthand pointed to an orange plastic chair outside the principal's door. "Have a seat," she said. "Mrs. Struggles will be with you in a few minutes."

"Have I done something wrong?" Bernadette asked.

Mrs. Shorthand eyed her as if she were a criminal. "Sit," she said. She turned away to answer the phone.

Bernadette settled into the chair, then opened her notebook. She reread her report about Mrs. Bozzetto.

Mrs. Shorthand whispered something into the phone's receiver.

Bernadette looked up from her notebook.

Stop the presses!

Had she just heard Mrs. Shorthand say the two most terrifying words that could ever be uttered in a school . . . *head lice*?

Bernadette's investigative heart leaped with joy.

Head lice were an even bigger scoop than crazy cat ladies!

Turning to a clean page in her notebook, she started writing.

But she'd only scrawled a few sentences when Mrs. Struggles opened her office door. She crooked her finger at Bernadette. "You and I need to have a little chat about cheese and truth, young lady."

Bernadette gulped and closed her notebook. Her report would have to wait until *after* detention.

The following Monday, the fifth graders were on the air again.

Melvin gave the announcements.

Ham read the menu.

Jackie reported on sports.

And Stanford droned on.

Then the camera panned to Bernadette. (Both the beauty and the joke segments had been canceled due to what Miss Turner called "the violent content of last week's reports.")

"Students of Aesop Elementary," said Bernadette gravely. "Last week, while in the office, I uncovered a disturbing revelation." She adjusted her horn-rimmed glasses, letting the suspense build, then said, "Our school is in the throes of a medical catastrophe—an outbreak of head lice." She paused, then concluded, "This reporter, for one, is grossed out. Aren't you?"

"Is it true?" gasped Missy as soon as the camera's Off light blinked red. "Is the school full of head lice?"

Bernadette shrugged. "Well, I think I overheard Mrs. Shorthand say it."

"You *think*?" repeated Humphrey.

"That's hearsay," said Amisha. "I know because my dad's an attorney."

"Whatever," replied Bernadette. She tucked her horn-rimmed glasses back into her pocket and headed to class.

That afternoon when the final bell rang, Mr.

Jupiter asked Bernadette to stay after school. "I want to talk to you about today's investigative report," he said.

"Hard-hitting, wasn't it?" bragged Bernadette.

"It certainly was," agreed Mr. Jupiter. "All afternoon, parents have flooded the office with calls demanding that action be taken. We've had exterminators in the basement, health inspectors in the lunchroom, and barbers calling in to offer their services."

Bernadette shrugged. "I report what I hear."

"And did you clearly hear Mrs. Shorthand say 'head lice'?"

Bernadette squirmed for a moment. "Maybe not *crystal* clearly," she finally admitted. "But I *think* that's what I heard her say."

Mr. Jupiter nodded. "Well, here are the facts as I know them. The school is implementing a new parking safety procedure. One suggestion was for teachers to drive off the lot with their *headlights* on."

"Oh," said Bernadette. "Oh . . . oh, no, I guess I'll be back in the principal's office tomorrow morning."

Mr. Jupiter patted her shoulder. "You know, when I worked as a cub reporter for the *Klondike Courier,* my editor was always shouting 'Dagnabbit it, Jupiter, verify your sources.'"

"I don't understand," said Bernadette.

"All good reporters verify their stories," explained Mr. Jupiter. "They don't just make things up based on hearsay and rumor. They interview people, double-check their facts, see for themselves. Do you understand?"

"I think so," said Bernadette.

"Good," said Mr. Jupiter with a smile. "Then I'll see you tomorrow."

Bernadette stuffed her notebook into her backpack and headed out to the bike ramp. But instead of pedaling straight home, she turned toward Vesta Street.

She braked in front of a gloomy old Victorian.

"It sure looks like the house of a crazy lady," muttered Bernadette.

At that moment the front door opened. Ms. Bozzetto stepped onto the porch in a cloud of felines—big cats, little cats, old cats, young cats, one-eyed cats, three-legged cats, striped cats, bald cats. They wove in and out of the art teacher's ankles, purring, mewing, and nipping.

"And that sure looks like a crazy cat lady."

Ms. Bozzetto waved. "Hello!" she called to Bernadette. "Have you come to adopt a cat?"

"Huh?" said Bernadette.

Ms. Bozzetto stomped her foot. "Isn't that a fine howdy-do—that blasted sign has fallen over again." Followed by the cats, she bounded into the yard, picked up the sign, and staked it back into the ground. The sign read:

MS. BOZZETTO'S HOME FOR FORLORN AND FORGOTTEN FELINES

Then she peered at Bernadette. "I know you!" she exclaimed. "You're that WUSS reporter."

Bernadette nodded.

"Can I help you with something?" asked Ms. Bozzetto. She bent and tickled a calico cat at her feet.

Bernadette nodded again. "I . . . I . . . was wondering if I could ask you a few questions," she stammered.

The art teacher beamed. "Sure," she said, holding open the gate. "Come on in."

The following Monday the fifth graders were on the air again—Melvin, Ham, Jackie, Stanford, and—

"Students of Aesop Elementary," said Bernadette in her most serious voice. "This reporter has uncovered evidence that a crazy woman works in our school."

Behind the camera, Ham groaned. "Not more rumors."

On camera, Bernadette said, "Her name is Ms. Bozzetto, our new art teacher, and she is crazy . . ." Bernadette adjusted her horn-rimmed glasses and rearranged her notes. "Crazy . . . about cats."

Behind Bernadette a picture appeared. It was of Ms. Bozzetto and Bernadette sitting on a hair-covered couch surrounded by a cloud of cats.

Bernadette smiled into the camera. "These are just a few of the forlorn and forgotten felines saved from the mean streets by Ms. Bozzetto's kindness and generosity. She takes them in—*all* of them—loves them, and cares for them until they are adopted by families of their own." Bernadette paused for effect. "This reporter, for one, is heart-warmed. Aren't you?"

MORAL: Don't believe everything you hear.

HYPERMIB...UM...HYPERMOB... UH...WEIRD BODY TRICKS

"LOOK WHAT I CAN DO!" ERNEST exclaimed during math. He cracked all ten of his knuckles.

"That's nothing," said Calvin. "Watch this!" He popped his thumbs out of joint.

"I've got you both beat," said Bernadette. She bent the fingers of her left hand all the way back until they touched her wrist.

Mr. Jupiter put down his protractor. "Those are all excellent examples of hypermobility," he said.

"Hyper-huh?" said Ham.

"Hypermobility," translated Stanford with a superior sniff. "It means having joints that stretch farther than normal."

"You mean like this?" asked Ham. He bent his arm behind his back and reached up to his ear.

"Precisely," said Mr. Jupiter.

"Can you do this?" asked Jackie. She touched the tip of her tongue to the tip of her nose.

Tongues wagged, but no one could.

"Or this?" asked Jackie. She touched the tip of her tongue to the point of her chin.

More wagging, but still no one could.

"Or this?" asked Jackie. She leaned forward and licked her own elbow.

Tongues around the room came up short.

Jackie raised her arms in victory. "The winner and fifth-grade hypermib . . . um . . . hypermob . . . uh . . . weird body tricks champion," she cried, "Jackie Jumpbaugh!" She made the sound of a roaring crowd.

"Big deal," said Lenny. "Even my dog can lick his own nose."

"And the other end too," added Bruce.

The two boys woofed and panted.

"Mongrels," said Victoria. She stuck out her tongue and then . . . folded it in half.

"Whoa!" exclaimed Ernest. "Did you see that?"

Everyone turned to Victoria.

"Do it again," urged Ernest.

Victoria did. Then she twisted her tongue into a basket shape . . . a clover shape . . . and then she rolled it up like a carpet.

"Who's champion now?" she asked.

"Pffft!" said Rachel. She stomped her foot for attention. "Pffft! Pffft! **Pffft!**"

The class looked at her.

"Pffft," said Rachel, and she moved her eyeballs back and forth, back and forth, faster and faster and faster still, until—

"Remarkable," commented Mr. Jupiter.

Rachel's eyeballs were shaking around in her head like a washing machine on the spin cycle.

The room erupted into a frenzy of weird body tricks as the fifth graders tried to outdo each other. Noses twitched. Joints popped. Skin stretched. Eyes crossed. Fingers tangled.

Ashley Z. burped the alphabet.

"At last," said Mr. Jupiter, nodding at the boy. "And it *was* worth the wait."

Now the fifth graders hollered at one another. "Try this!"

"Can you do this?"

"Watch me!"

Only Melvin remained in his seat. He silently watched his classmates with a bemused look on his face.

For the first time, Calvin noticed him.

"What's the matter with you?" Calvin asked. "Don't you know any tricks?"

"I know some," said Melvin.

"They must not be any good if you're not showing them off," said Calvin.

Melvin shrugged. "They're okay."

The others noticed Melvin too.

"I bet yours are nothing compared to my knuckle trick," said Ernest.

"Or my tongue trick," said Victoria.

Mr. Jupiter turned to Melvin and nodded encouragingly. "Share with us," he said.

"Okay, if you really want me to," said Melvin. He pushed off his shoes, stripped off his socks, and padded barefoot to the front of the room.

The class stopped and watched.

And Melvin sneezed . . . but his eyes stayed open!

"That's it?" said Calvin. "That's your trick?"

"There's more," replied Melvin.

Plucking a kazoo off Mr. Jupiter's desk, he played "America the Beautiful." As he did, he raised his eyebrows, first the left one, then the right one, then the left one, then the right one. Left, right. Left, right. His eyebrows kept time to the song's beat.

"Interesting," admitted Calvin.

"There's more," said Melvin.

Dropping the kazoo back onto the desk, he sat on the floor. Then he bent his left index finger all the way back to his wrist. He crooked his left arm all the way behind his back. He wrapped his left leg behind his neck, tucked his elbow behind his knee, and let his left foot dangle over his right shoulder.

Eyes wide, Bernadette pulled out her reporter's notebook.

"I don't believe it!" exclaimed Calvin.

"There's more," said Melvin. This time he bent his right index finger all the way back to his wrist. He crooked his right arm all the way behind his back. He wrapped his right leg behind his neck, tucked his elbow behind his knee, and let his right foot dangle over his left shoulder.

Emberly, who had spent his summer reading the entire McFardy Boys mystery series, pulled out his magnifying glass for a closer look.

"He's a human pretzel," declared Calvin.

"There's more," said Melvin. Rolling head over elbow down the aisle, he pushed up his desk lid with his head and fished around until he pulled out his lunch bag with his teeth. Then, using just his bare toes, he unwrapped the straw from his juice box. For several seconds all anyone could see were his lips and cheeks moving as he sucked the juice into his mouth. Then—

TA-DA!

Melvin stuck out his tongue. On its tip was the straw, and it was—

"Tied in a knot!" shouted Calvin. "He tied a knot with his tongue."

The classroom exploded into whistles and cheers and applause.

Even Mr. Jupiter whooped. "I haven't seen anything that extraordinary since my traveling days with those famous Venetian contortionists, the Tumbling Twistolinis."

Melvin unfolded himself. "It was nothing," he said with a blush.

"Nothing?" repeated Humphrey.

"Why, you're a genius . . . a master!" cried Calvin. "Geez, you should have told us you could do all that years ago. We'd have noticed you back in first grade."

The others nodded in agreement.

Then Jackie pretended she was talking into a microphone. "Here he is, sports fans, the fifth-grade hypermib . . . hypermob . . . weird body tricks champion—Melvin Moody!" She made the sound of a roaring crowd.

"Gee, thanks," said Melvin. He sat back down at his desk and put his shoes and socks on.

MORAL: He who does a thing well does not have to boast.

CLASS PETS

ONE MORNING IN OCTOBER, MR. SWILL huffed and wheezed and struggled down the hall with a big wooden crate. He pushed open Mr. Jupiter's door with his foot.

The class looked up from their *One Hundred and Ninety-two Countries Everyone Should Know* textbooks.

"Good morning!" chirped Mr. Jupiter.

"Heavy," grunted Mr. Swill. "Heavy." Stumbling into the classroom, he lowered the crate to the floor, then fell back against the totem pole, gasping for breath.

Mr. Jupiter read the postmark on the crate. "Burma," he said. He smiled. "Good, they've finally arrived."

"Finally arrived?" repeated Humphrey. "What's finally arrived?"

"Our class pets," replied Mr. Jupiter.

At the word *pets*, the fifth graders leaped from their seats and crowded around the crate. Even Mr. Swill found the energy to look interested.

"Do you think it's a unicorn?" squealed Ashlee A. and Ashleigh B. They clutched each other's arms with excitement, then broke into a cheer: "Unicorns! Unicorns! GOOOOO, Unicorns!"

Ashley Z. covered his ears. "I hope it's a girl-eating Siberian tiger."

"Or a rare and exotic pink-headed duck," said Lenny. "I read about those in *International Geographic*."

"Hey!" cried Bruce. "What do you call the tiger who swallowed the duck?"

The others stared at him.

"A duck-filled-fatty-pus!"

Lenny and Bruce high-fived and howled with laughter.

"Why don't we just open the crate and find out?" suggested Emberly.

"Excellent idea," said Mr. Jupiter. Grabbing the battle-ax off the suit of armor, he raised it over his head.

"Wait!" cried Rose. "There are words written on this side."

"What do they say?" asked Mr. Jupiter.

Rose peered at the words. She read aloud: "'Elusive in nature.'"

"Huh?" said Ham. "What's that mean?"

Stanford rolled his eyes. "Elusive means hard to find," he translated.

"You mean like an ivory-billed woodpecker?" asked Ham.

"Or a giant squid?" said Bernadette.

"Hurry, Mr. Jupiter, open it!" exclaimed Amisha. She crossed her legs and bounced from foot to foot. "The suspense is going to make me *e-x-p-l-o-d-e*!"

Using the ax, Mr. Jupiter carefully pried off the lid. Everyone peered inside to see . . .

"Another box!" exclaimed Emberly.

They pulled the second, smaller box out of the first.

"This one has writing too," said Rose. She ran her finger under the words, and—leaving an ink smudge behind—she read: "'Strange and unique.'"

"Strange and unique," repeated Humphrey. "Our pets are strange and unique."

"*And* elusive in nature," Stanford reminded him.

"I wonder if they have fangs and breathe fire," said Melvin.

Calvin grinned at his new friend. "That'd be way cool."

"Open it, Mr. Jupiter," begged Amisha. She crossed her legs, bounced from foot to foot, and swayed back and forth. "Open it, *p-l-e-a-s-e*."

"Pretty pleeeeeease," snickered Lenny.

"Before she peeees," giggled Bruce.

Mr. Jupiter pried the lid off the second box. Everyone peeked inside to find . . .

"Another box!" cried Emberly.

They pulled the third, even smaller box out of the second.

This one read: FROM THE ENDS OF THE EARTH.

"Let me open it," begged Mr. Swill, who had finally caught his breath. His hands shaking with excitement, he pulled a large screwdriver from his tool belt and jimmied the lid off the third box.

Everyone looked inside to find . . .

"Another box," moaned Emberly.

"I gotta *g-o*!" squealed Amisha. She dashed out the door as the others pulled the fourth, smallest box out of the third.

It read: COME THE CREATURES YOU SEEK.

"What creatures?" wondered Ham. "What could live in there?"

"Whatever they are, they must be as tiny as scorpions to fit in that little space," noted Rose.

"And quiet," said Missy, pressing her ear against the box. "I haven't heard a single hiss or growl."

"And poetic," said Lil. "Listen." And she recited,

> *"Elusive in nature,*
> *Strange and unique,*
> *From the ends of the earth*
> *Come the creatures you seek."*

She sighed. "Isn't that a lovely verse?"

"That's not a poem, those are clues," corrected Emberly. He whipped out his magnifying glass. "We must decipher the clues and discover what lies deep within this box."

"Or," said Mr. Jupiter, "we could just open it."

With Mr. Swill's help, he pulled the lid off the fourth box.

"I hope they don't bite," said Ashlee A.

"I hope they don't fly," said Ashleigh B.

"I hope they don't stink," said Ashley Z.

The class took a step back as Mr. Jupiter reached into the fourth box and pulled out . . .

A cage with a card attached.

The card read: GUINEA PIGS.

A deflated silence filled the room.

Then Emberly cried, "Guinea pigs? That's it? Guinea pigs?"

"What a bust," sniffed Mr. Swill. Snatching back his screwdriver, he stomped out the door.

"We wanted a unicorn!" wailed Ashlee A. and Ashleigh B. in unison.

"But these are Burmese spectacled guinea pigs," said Mr. Jupiter. He held the cage (complete with food, water, and exercise wheel) high so everyone could see the two beady-eyed, brown-spotted creatures huddled in one corner.

"Get serious," snorted Stanford. "Guinea pigs are guinea pigs."

Lenny stepped up for a closer look. "I don't see any-thing special about them. They look exactly like my third-grade guinea pigs, which looked exactly like my second-grade guinea pigs, which looked exactly like my first-grade guinea pigs, which looked exactly like my kindergarten guinea pigs, which looked exactly like— you got it!—my preschool guinea pigs."

Victoria gave her hair a flip. "Really, Mr. Jupiter, I thought you were more original than this. Guinea pigs? Dull-o-rama."

"Victoria's right," said Calvin. "All guinea pigs do is eat, sleep, poop, and escape. End of story."

The fifth graders turned their backs on the guinea pigs and flopped back into their seats.

"I see," said Mr. Jupiter. Without saying another word, he set the cage on the back table between a scale model of the Taj Mahal and a camarasaurus skull, then picked up the teacher's copy of *One Hundred and Ninety-two Countries Everyone Should Know*.

Just then Amisha burst into the classroom. "What did we get?" she cried. "A Komodo dragon? A two-headed cobra? A dodo bird?"

"Guinea pigs," grumbled Emberly. "We got guinea pigs."

"Oh, no," sobbed Amisha, crossing her legs and bouncing from foot to foot. "Here comes my disappointment." She dashed out the door again.

Mr. Jupiter studied his students' crestfallen faces for a moment, then said, "Let's continue with our study of countries, shall we? When we left off, we were learning about Austria. Let's review. Rose, what is its capital city?"

"Vienna," moped Rose.

"Yes," said Mr. Jupiter. "And what is its official language, Humphrey?"

"German," pouted Humphrey.

"Correct," said Mr. Jupiter. "And who, Melvin, is the country's most famous musician?"

"Wolfgang Amadeus Mozart," sulked Melvin.

"That's right," said Mr. Jupiter. "Now, class, please take out your kazoos. Together we're going to play the allegro from Mozart's Serenade Number Thirteen for Strings in G major, more commonly known as 'A Little Night Music.'"

Grudgingly, the children dug their kazoos out of their desks. They raised the kazoos somberly to their lips.

"And a-one, and a-two, and a-blow that kazoo!"

The classroom filled with the halfhearted strains of Mozart's famous first chords: "*La,* la *la,* la *la* la la la laaaa . . ."

And in their cage, the guinea pigs rose up on their hind legs, threw back their brown-spotted heads, and answered in high-pitched squeaky song: "*Eek*, eek *eek*, eek *eek* eek eek eek eeeek . . ."

"Whoa! Did you hear that?" asked Calvin.

"I heard it, but I don't believe it," answered Emberly.

"Let's play the next line," suggested Rose.

With more gusto this time, the fifth graders played, "Dum dum, *da* da da da da daaaa . . ."

And with the same extraordinary singing voices, the guinea pigs replied, "Eek eek, *eek* eek eek eek eek eeeek . . ."

Their enthusiasm at full throttle now, the fifth graders really belted it out. "Da *da*, da da da da daaaa . . ."

The guinea pigs belted it back. "Eek *eek*, eek eek eek eeek . . ."

At the front of the room, Mr. Jupiter snatched up a fossil rib unearthed during a paleontological dig in eastern Uzbekistan. Waving the bone like a conductor's baton, he cried, "All together now!"

On the downbeat, guinea pigs and kazoos melded into one joyous, melodious, wondrous concert.

"Wow!" whispered Rachel when the music finally faded away.

"Did you just say something?" asked Ham.

"Pffft," replied Rachel. "Just pffft."

"That's what I thought you said," said Ham.

Rose shyly raised her hand. "Um . . . Mr. Jupiter, did you know Burmese spectacled guinea pigs are . . . um . . . musical?"

"Very musical," he replied. "They may be the most musical creatures in all of nature, able to squeak any tune, from Mozart to Motown, with perfect pitch. The incredible thing about them is that once they hear a song, they never forget it. And since Burmese spectacled guinea pigs can live longer than a hundred years, their repertoire of songs can be infinite."

"Like an MP3 player!" exclaimed Lenny. "Call them gPods!"

Mr. Jupiter grinned. "Something like that."

Everyone crowded around the cage to take a closer look at the new class pets.

Just then Amisha burst back into the classroom. "Why are you all standing around that cage? Ugh! Guinea pigs are so *b-o-r-i-n-g*."

Emberly smiled. "That's what *you* think."

And raising their kazoos to their lips, the fifth graders began to play . . .

MORAL: Appearances can be deceiving.

LET IT RAIN

ON THE WEDNESDAY AFTER Thanksgiving break, the fifth graders arrived at school to find Mr. Jupiter—

"Gone!" gasped Missy.

"This is a case for Emberly Everclass!" declared Emberly. He closed his latest McFardy Boys mystery, pulled out his magnifying glass, and began examining the teacher's desk for clues.

"Get serious," snorted Stanford. "He's probably just late."

"*You* get serious," replied Emberly. "He's *never* late."

At that moment, the door burst open and Mr. Jupiter bustled in, carrying a cardboard box. "Everyone, please take your seats," he called out.

The fifth graders sat.

"Forgive my tardiness," Mr. Jupiter continued as he dropped the box on his desk, "but I had a minor crisis at home. My fifteen-inch telescope with Cassegrain focus and thirty-six-segment primary mirror—the one

I just had installed—came crashing in through my roof this morning. Can you believe it?" He shook his head. "I had lens bits everywhere, and the eyepiece landed right on top of my collection of rare and ancient books and manuscripts. Luckily, they were unharmed." He patted the box. "They should be safe here until the roof can be repaired."

The students watched as Mr. Jupiter pushed back the box's flaps and pulled out leather-bound volumes trimmed in gold, medieval illuminated manuscripts, clay tablets covered with cuneiform writing, and fragile papyrus scrolls.

Sweeping aside the class copies of *Cooking with Pooh Without Making a Piglet of Yourself*, Mr. Jupiter carefully arranged his collection in its new place on the shelf. Then he wiped his hands on his lederhosen—the pair he had bought during his goat-herding seminar in the Alps—and turned to face the class.

"Do not touch these," he said.

In the back row, Ham felt a sudden urge to unroll scrolls, touch cuneiform markings, run his finger along exotic spines.

"Not only are they rare and valuable," continued Mr. Jupiter with reverence, "but they contain the secrets of the ancient world—knowledge you are not yet old enough to comprehend."

In the back row, Ham longed to peek between the fine leather covers.

"So, fifth graders," concluded Mr. Jupiter with a slight smile, "hands off."

In the back row, Ham shivered with excitement. He couldn't wait to get his hands on the collection.

His chance came at lunchtime.

Cook had already heaped Ham's tray with seven-layer cranberry loaf (she was still getting rid of last week's leftovers) when he slapped his forehead. "I left my lunch pass in my desk!" he cried.

Cook snatched back her food. "Go get it," she said. "But be quick about it. Cranberry loaf is a dish best served hot."

Ham hurried back to the now-empty classroom. He rummaged around in his desk, pulled out his pass, and . . .

MR. JUPITER'S COLLECTION!

For the first time in his life, literature pushed lunch right out of Ham's head. He moved toward the shelf. Glancing furtively around, he pulled down a volume. It was thick and heavy and its centuries-old cover smelled of dust and secrets. Ham peered at the book's title, written in faded gold leaf:

The Babylonian Book of Babble: An Ancient Primer.

It opened with a creak.

On page four Ham found a chart labeled "Pyramids and Ziggurats Made Easy."

On page seventy-six he found instructions titled "How to Weed Your Hanging Gardens."

And on page one thousand and three he found an illuminated engraving of a thunderstorm, complete with black clouds, flashing lightning, floods, and hail. Beneath the engraving were the words *Yawa og niar niar.*

I wonder what that's about? thought Ham. He muttered the words aloud to himself. *"Yawa og niar niar."*

A wispy gray rain cloud suddenly appeared above his head.

Drip-drop.

The cloud squeezed out a thimbleful of water, then—

Poof!

It dissipated.

"No way!" gasped Ham, wiping the trickle of rainwater from his cheek.

Then he said the words again. "*Yawa og niar niar.*"

This time a slightly bigger, slightly darker cloud appeared. Ham pointed to the Venus flytrap sitting on the windowsill.

The cloud obeyed.

It glided across the room, stopped above the plant, and . . .

Dribble-dribble-pitter-plop!

. . . produced a light drizzle.

The Venus flytrap snapped angrily at the raindrops.

Poof!

The second cloud dissipated just like the first.

Ham let the truth sink in. Then—

"I've got the power!" he sang at the top of his voice. He danced around and punched the air. "The power . . . the power . . . whooo . . . whooo . . . . whooo!"

In their cage, the Burmese spectacled guinea pigs sang back in perfect harmony. "Eeeek . . . . eeeek . . . . eeeek!"

"I can't wait to show Humphrey!" exclaimed Ham. Without bothering to read the rest of the page, he slid the book back onto the shelf and bolted for the lunch-room.

But in the doorway, he skittered to a stop.

Mrs. Bunz was on a rampage.

"Who put their leftover soup in the recycling bin?" the lunchroom monitor bellowed into her bullhorn. Plucking out the offending bowl, she held it high for everyone to see, then poured it into a bucket of slop at her feet. "Who's responsible for this irresponsibility?"

Cowering, the students stared nervously down at their corn chips and carrot sticks.

And Ham whispered, "*Yawa og niar niar.*"

The cloud materialized, a bit bigger and a bit darker than before.

Feeling powerful, Ham pointed at the lunchroom monitor.

The cloud stormed across the lunchroom. It snatched the hairnet from Mrs. Bunz's head. It ripped the apron from her ample hips. It grabbed the bullhorn from her tight fist and sent it skittering. Then—

SPLASH!

It drenched her with a cloudburst, and—

Poof!

It was gone.

A stunned silence fell over the lunchroom. Then—

"I always knew Mrs. Bunz was all wet!" cried Bruce.

The place exploded in loud, roaring laughter that echoed all the way to the teachers' lounge.

"Do you hear that?" asked Mrs. Gluteal, her cake-laden fork stopping in midair. "It sounds like a riot."

Mrs. Chen nodded in agreement. "Perhaps one of us should go and see what's happening," she suggested.

"Before someone makes a mess," agreed Mr. Swill.

"Or gets hurt," added Nurse Betadine.

"Or earns a detention," said Mrs. Struggles.

The teachers looked at one another for a moment.

Then Mrs. Gluteal held up her plate. "Cake, anyone?"

In the lunchroom, a now dripping wet Mrs. Bunz whirled on the students. "Who did that?"

No one answered.

Mrs. Bunz's eyes became slits. "You haven't heard the last of this," she warned. "I'll ferret out the culprit. I'll find you. And when I do? Five minutes—*on the wall*!"

On the wall!

It was Mrs. Bunz's favorite punishment—a unique form of torture involving a public apology and five long, humiliating minutes against the cold tiles of the lunchroom wall.

On the wall!

Those three little words caused everyone—first through fifth grade alike—to freeze.

Perhaps, decided Ham with a shudder, *I should keep my new powers a secret.*

That afternoon, Mr. Jupiter said, "I understand something very unusual took place in the lunchroom today." He studied each of his students' faces. "Does anyone know what happened?"

"I believe it was simply one of life's mysteries," said Lil. And she waxed poetic:

> *"Ah! Sweet mystery of life, at last I've found thee.*
> *Ah! At last I know the secret of it all. . . ."*

"No mystery should go unexplained," said Emberly. "Arty McFardy says—"

Stanford interrupted with a snort. "Get serious. There is a logical and scientific explanation for what happened."

Mr. Jupiter looked around the room. "Does anyone *have* that explanation?"

The classroom fell silent.

In the back row, Ham plastered an innocent look on his face.

"One last question," said Mr. Jupiter. "Who watered the Venus flytrap? It's been spitting and sputtering since lunchtime."

The classroom stayed silent.

"Anyone?" persisted Mr. Jupiter.

"Pa-tooey!" coughed the flytrap.

Disappointed, Mr. Jupiter shook his head. "If no one will answer my question, then I guess we'll just have to move on." Picking up a stack of papers, he began handing them out. "I hope you all did your zoology reading last night, because we're having a pop quiz."

Ham leaned forward. "Zoology reading?" he whispered in Victoria's ear. "I didn't even know we had a zoology book."

"Too bad for you," she replied with a flip of her hair.

Ham gulped and read the first question: "Bactrian camels have two humps. What is a one-humped camel called?"

Ham had no idea. Guessing, he wrote, "Humphrey."

He moved on to the second question: "What do ducks do in the fall when food is scarce?"

Ham guessed again. "Go to the store and say, 'Put it on my bill.'"

He read the third question: "What animal has three heads and smells bad?"

Ham wrote, "Victoria," but he knew that wasn't right. He was pretty sure his first two answers weren't right either. As for the next ninety-seven questions? He didn't have a clue.

He did, however, have the power.

"Yawa og niar niar."

A cloud materialized, the biggest and darkest of them all.

Ham made a swirling motion with his hand.

Instantly, a cool mist of rain swirled around the fifth graders, tickling their faces and freckling their test papers.

Ashley Z. peeled off his shoes and socks and splashed in the little puddles that began to form on the floor, while Lil and the Burmese spectacled guinea pigs burst into a squeaky rendition of "Singin' in the Rain."

"So much for zoology," smirked Ham. Feeling powerful, he signaled for the cloud to stop.

Instead, it turned darker. Thunder rumbled. Lightning flashed. The gentle mist turned into stinging, slashing rain.

"Take cover!" shouted Mr. Jupiter. Braving the storm, he raced back and forth between the bookshelf containing his collection and a nearby Byzantine funeral chest. When the last manuscript was safe, he dove in on top of them. The fifth graders ducked beneath their desks.

"What's happening?" cried Calvin. He fumbled in his desk for a pencil to chew on.

"Mr. Jupiter," begged Ernest. "Make it stop!"

From inside the chest, Mr. Jupiter called out, "I can't control the weather."

Even though he couldn't see Mr. Jupiter's eyes, Ham swore he could feel them boring into him. "Please, cloud, stop now," Ham begged.

But the cloud turned darker still. It whirled. It

churned. It snatched the test papers off the desks and spun them around and around.

"Hey!" Stanford shouted at the cloud. "No copying!" He tried to grab his test back.

ZAP!

The cloud shot him a warning flash of lightning.

"Yow!" cried Stanford.

Ham was whimpering now. "Please stop, cloud. Pretty please with hot fudge and tuna on top."

Instead, it hailed. Balls of ice pinged and popped and bounced across the classroom. They put a dent in the suit of armor. They dimpled the Zulu war shield. They bruised Rachel's head.

"Ouchie!" she cried.

Beneath his desk, Ham felt powerless. He burst into tears.

"It's my fault," he wailed at the top of his voice. "I touched Mr. Jupiter's rare books. I read the ancient words. I learned how to turn the cloud on, but I didn't learn how to turn it off."

Mr. Jupiter poked his head out of the chest. "Thank you for your honesty, Ham," he shouted over the hailstorm.

"Honesty schmonesty," hollered Missy. "Who'll stop the rain?"

"If I recall correctly," cried Mr. Jupiter, "page XXIV of the *Babylonian Book of Babble* clearly states that to reverse the curse one must reverse the verse." A golf-ball-sized piece of hail smacked him on the head. "But I may be mistaken."

"Huh?" said Ham. "Reverse the verse?"

As the ice balls bounced around him, Ham pondered Mr. Jupiter's words. Reverse the verse. Reverse the curse.

And then it struck him!

Yawa og niar niar backwards was . . .

"Rain, rain, go away!" shouted Ham.

And at that, the hail stopped. The cloud disappeared. And the test papers floated back down to the desktops.

"Thank you, Ham," said Mr. Jupiter, climbing out of the chest and squeezing water from his Sumerian bow tie. "Is everyone all right?"

The soggy students sputtered and nodded just as the final bell rang.

"We'll finish our quizzes tomorrow," said Mr. Jupiter. "Once they've dried off."

Nodding again, the students sloshed toward the door.

"Hold on a minute, Ham," said Mr. Jupiter. "Where do you think you're going?"

"Home?" replied Ham.

Mr. Jupiter shook his head. "You'll be going to the broom closet," he said.

"Huh?" said Ham.

"That's where the mop and bucket are kept," added Mr. Jupiter.

"Oh," said Ham. "I get it."

For the next hour, Ham mopped and wrung and sponged. He toweled off the guinea pigs; he squeezed out the Venus flytrap; he polished the suit of armor until there wasn't a water spot on it. But he steered well clear of the shelf where Mr. Jupiter's collection of rare and ancient books and manuscripts once again sat.

"I'm keeping my hands off," he told himself.

MORAL: A little knowledge is a dangerous thing.

A HISTORY LESSON

AS HE HAD EVERY FRIDAY MORNING
since the school year began, Mr. Jupiter said, "Let's begin by reviewing some American history. I trust everyone read last night's assignment?"

And as always, Bernadette fidgeted.

Melvin ducked his head behind his left knee.

And Calvin quickly looked at Stanford. "I bet the human computer did."

Stanford turned as red as the Mongolian caftan Mr. Jupiter was wearing. "I . . . um . . . I . . . uh . . . was so absorbed in my philatelic studies, I ran out of time."

"Huh?" said Ham.

"My stamp collection," translated Stanford.

"Oh," said Ham. "I get it."

Mr. Jupiter sighed. "Didn't anyone study their history lesson last night?"

No one raised a hand.

"Then I guess there's no reason to talk about these," said Mr. Jupiter. He whisked a black cloth off his desk to reveal a set of big yellow teeth. A jumble of rusting wires and rotting springs held the teeth together.

"Ewww, what's that?" asked Missy.

"George Washington's dentures," replied Mr. Jupiter. "They were given to me by the International Tooth and Gum Association for inventing floss-on-a-stick."

The children gathered around for a closer look.

"I didn't know George Washington wore dentures," Ham finally said.

Mr. Jupiter nodded. "Poor George had terrible teeth. They kept rotting and falling out, rotting and falling out. By the time he became president, he only had one tooth remaining in his mouth. That's why he had to wear dentures."

"Is that true?" asked Lenny. He poked the teeth suspiciously. "These don't look like my grandpa's dentures."

"Of course they don't," said Mr. Jupiter. "There weren't any modern dental methods back then, so people had to make dentures out of some pretty odd things. Washington's dentures are made from cow and hippopotamus teeth."

Lenny rolled his eyes. "You're telling me that

George Washington walked around with hippo in his mouth? I don't believe it."

Mr. Jupiter shrugged. "No? Then I guess there's no reason to talk about *this,* either." He pulled a long ivory toothbrush out of his desk drawer.

"I suppose you're going to tell me *that's* George Washington's toothbrush," sniffed Lenny.

"No," replied Mr. Jupiter. "I'm going to tell you that this is George Washington's *horses'* toothbrush."

"Huh?" said Ham.

"Our first president obviously learned from his dental mistakes," explained Mr. Jupiter. "On his orders, each of his six white horses had its teeth brushed every morning. According to Martha Washington, the horses' breath smelled better than her husband's."

Everyone laughed but Lenny.

"I don't think that's very funny, Mr. Jupiter!" he cried. "You shouldn't make up historical facts."

"How do you know they're made up?" asked Mr. Jupiter.

"Because history is boring," answered Lenny. "There's no laughing in history."

"Sure there is," replied Mr. Jupiter. "History is full of funny stories, as well as daring adventures and

74

heroic deeds." He sighed. "Of course, you won't read your book." He shook his head. "That's so sad."

He let his words sink in a moment before clapping his hands. "Everyone return to your desks and take out your rock picks. It's time for mineralogy."

Lenny shrugged and slid back into his chair. Opening the lid of his desk, he peered past his spitball collection and rubber tarantula to the never-opened history book in back.

"Funny stories, huh?" he muttered to himself.

Using his rock pick to excavate the book, he slipped it into his backpack.

MORAL: Incentive spurs effort.

NOTES TO YOU

MR. HALFNOTE WAS WORRIED.

"Ever since they returned from winter break, the fifth graders simply refuse to take music class seriously," he admitted to the other teachers during lunch one day. He told them about the previous week's lesson, on breathing and posture.

"Sit up straight and tall, but relaxed," Mr. Halfnote had instructed the class.

Instantly, the fifth graders had started giggling and wiggling and slip-sliding out of their chairs. Music stands toppled. Sheet music scattered. Brasses and woodwinds rolled across the floor.

"Stop!" Mr. Halfnote had hollered. "What do you think you're doing?"

"We're trying to sit up straight and tall, *butt* relaxed," replied Lenny.

"But we just can't seem to get to the *bottom* of it," added Bruce.

The rest of the students had shrieked with laughter.

Mr. Halfnote had spent the rest of the hour trying to regain control of his class.

"That is terrible," Miss Turner agreed when he finished his story. She patted him sympathetically on the back.

"It gets worse," confessed Mr. Halfnote. And he described that morning's lesson.

"Today, as we accompany ourselves on our zithers, we're going to learn the chorus from 'The Battle Hymn of the Republic,'" Mr. Halfnote had instructed the class. "Ready?"

Lenny had grinned. "We're always ready."

"Then instruments up," said Mr. Halfnote. "Annnd begin."

The fifth graders had plucked and bowed. Above the screeching racket, Mr. Halfnote could just make out the chorus's lyrics:

> *"Glory, glory hallelujah!*
> *Don't let the teachers try to fool ya.*
> *There's a dungeon 'neath the floor*
> *With a padlock on the door*
> *And you won't see the kids no more."*

The "Battle Hymn" had three verses. By the time the students had finished singing, Mr. Halfnote's head was throbbing.

"Awful, just awful," said Mrs. Gluteal. She handed him a caramel drop cookie as consolation.

Mr. Halfnote took a sad little bite. "It is," he sighed. "It truly is. After all, music is a universal language. It allows children to express themselves. But most importantly, playing together, creating music as a group, is transformative. It can change their lives."

"I couldn't agree more," said Miss Turner.

"So what can I do to motivate them?" asked Mr. Halfnote.

"Have you tried a gold star chart?" chirped Miss Fairchild. "My kindergartners *love* gold stars."

"Or the promise of a pizza party," suggested Mrs. Chen. "Kids can't resist pepperoni."

"What about a field trip?" said Mr. Jupiter. "Who wouldn't fall in love with music after hearing the Blinkendorf Symphony Orchestra performing the overture from *Der Wienerdog*?"

"Ah, the BSO," said Miss Turner with a sigh. "It brings back memories, doesn't it, Harry?"

Mr. Jupiter smiled and touched the librarian's hand.

"Money," blurted out Mr. Swill, who had been mopping around the coffee machine. "Money's the best motivator. You think I'd clean one square foot of this place if I didn't get a paycheck?"

The others laughed.

But Mr. Halfnote leaped to his feet. "Cornelius!" he exclaimed, grabbing the janitor's mop and dancing it around the room. "You're brilliant!" He dashed out the door.

For the next week—with the help of Ms. Bozzetto's printing press—Mr. Halfnote made money. Each bill was decorated with musical symbols—treble clefs, breath marks, bar lines. And in the center, each sported a smiling likeness of the music teacher.

"I call them musical notes," Mr. Halfnote told the fifth graders at their next lesson. "You can earn them by participating in class and exhibiting good behavior."

"Why would we want to do that?" asked Lenny. "What can we do with fake money?"

"You can shop at my emporium," replied Mr. Halfnote.

"Huh?" said Ham.

"Store," translated Stanford, rolling his eyes. "Emporium means store."

"And here it is," said Mr. Halfnote. He pushed into the center of the room a long table loaded with Chinese yo-yos, flashing finger lights, temporary tattoos, rubber spiders, McFardy Boys notebooks, and much, much more. Some of the items on the table, like the jawbreakers, cost only one note. Other items, like the stuffed toy unicorn, cost a whopping twenty notes.

"I want *that*," Ashlee A. whispered to Ashleigh B.

Mr. Halfnote went on with his explanation. "Every few weeks, I will open the emporium. At that time, those of you who have earned musical notes may spend them."

Calvin raised his hand. "Do we have to spend our notes right away, or can we save them?"

"You may spend as little or as much as you like," replied Mr. Halfnote. "You can save up for more expensive items."

He paused, allowing the students to admire his wares. Then he handed each of them a wallet made of brown construction paper. Each wallet contained one musical note. "To start you off," explained Mr. Halfnote.

"Can I buy something now?" begged Ham. He eyed the chocolate insects. "Mmmm . . . choco-roaches."

"Not today," said Mr. Halfnote.

"When *can* we shop?" asked Ham.

Mr. Halfnote grinned. "Whenever I decide to open the emporium."

"But doesn't your store have set business hours?" said Victoria. "All stores have set business hours."

"Not this one," said Mr. Halfnote. "You'll just have to earn and wait."

Lenny thought a moment, then hurried to his chair. "Look at me, Mr. Halfnote," he sang out. "I'm sitting up straight and tall . . . but relaxed."

Mr. Halfnote grinned again. "Leonard," he said, "your exemplary behavior has just earned you a musical note."

Lenny preened as the others, too, sat straight and tall in their chairs.

For the rest of the hour the class learned about melody and harmony. No one fell on the floor or sang funny song lyrics.

Over the next few weeks, Missy stopped losing her music book and instead came to class with it tucked securely under her arm.

She earned two notes *and* learned to read music.

Rose volunteered to play the broken triangle—the one nobody wanted because it was missing the little metal piece to play it with (Mr. Halfnote used an old spoon from the lunchroom).

She earned three notes *and* discovered a natural talent for percussion.

Humphrey took it upon himself to empty all the trumpets' spit valves.

He earned seven notes . . .

Mr. Halfnote noticed Humphrey's saliva-speckled shirt.

"Make that eight notes," said the music teacher.

. . . *and* increased his finger dexterity.

"Who knew music could be so much fun?" Missy said to Rose one afternoon as they headed back to their classroom.

"It *is* the universal language," replied Rose.

"YES!" Mr. Halfnote whispered victoriously to himself.

By the time the music teacher finally opened the

emporium for business, the students' wallets, as well as their minds, were full.

"What to buy?" Ernest asked himself. He walked around and around the table, picking up an item, examining it, putting it down, picking up an item, examining it, putting it down, picking up an item . . .

Ham made a decisive purchase.

CRUNCH!

"*OWWW!*

"Mmmm," he sighed happily, "jawbreakers."

Lenny and Bruce combined their earnings and bought a whoopee cushion.

"We consider it an investment in our comedic futures," explained Lenny.

"Yeah, we're starting with the classics," added Bruce, eyeing the puddle of rubber vomit.

For a few minutes, the music room bubbled with excitement as the fifth graders made their choices and handed over their notes.

Only Calvin remained seated.

"Aren't you going to buy anything?" asked Ashlee A. She hugged her new stuffed unicorn.

"Nope," replied Calvin. "I'm just going to earn and save."

And that was exactly what he did.

Over the next weeks, Calvin earned:

Two notes for passing out sheet music.

Four notes for attempting to play "Lady of Spain" on the accordion.

Three notes for attempting to play "Yellow Bird" on the accordion.

Ten notes for promising not to play *anything* on the accordion.

His construction-paper wallet grew so thick with notes, he had to ask Mr. Halfnote for another.

"Wow," commented Humphrey. "You must really love music."

"Who cares about music?" replied Calvin. "It's the *notes* I love."

And he kept earning:

Three notes for waxing the xylophone.

Eight notes for learning the correct verses to "The Battle Hymn of the Republic."

Sixteen notes for tutoring Lenny on the kazoo.

By the time Mr. Halfnote's emporium opened for business again, Calvin had—

"A hundred notes!" exclaimed Humphrey. "I bet you have a hundred notes."

Calvin, who had retired to a corner of the music room so he could be alone with his money, nodded proudly.

"What are you going to buy?" asked Humphrey.

"Nothing."

"Nothing? But you could buy a glow-in-the-dark calculator, or a carton of number two pencils, or . . . or . . ."

Calvin shuddered. He didn't want any of that stuff. All he wanted was notes—lots and lots of notes. He desired them. He craved them. His greatest joy was to earn them so he could watch his stack grow . . . and grow . . . and grow.

"You do know that it's fake money," Humphrey reminded him.

"Uh-huh," said Calvin vaguely. He arranged his notes into stacks of ten.

"You can't do anything with it except shop at Mr. Halfnote's store," persisted Humphrey.

"Uh-huh," said Calvin again. He rearranged his notes into stacks of twenty.

"So what's the point of saving it?" asked Humphrey.

Calvin stopped stacking. He looked up. "It makes me happy," he said.

"Happy?" repeated Humphrey.

"Happy," said Calvin.

"Uh-huh," said Humphrey. Rolling his eyes, he walked away.

Calvin went back to stacking, counting, and sorting his notes.

That afternoon, after music, Mr. Jupiter worked with the children on word problems. "Let's see how many of you can solve this one," he said.

At the word *solve*, Calvin stuck a pencil in his mouth and started gnawing. He couldn't help it. When he was nervous, he chewed. And math—his very worst subject—made him very, very nervous.

At the front of the room, Mr. Jupiter continued. "A troll named Igor bought his sister, Griselda, three bottles of Wart-Away costing twenty-four dollars each, and his other sister, Esmeralda, five bottles of Hair-Today-Gone-Tomorrow at eighteen dollars each. How much money did Igor spend on beauty aids for his sisters?"

At his desk, Calvin chomped and chewed and thought about his notes. He saw himself stacking, sorting, counting . . . twenty-four dollars . . . eighteen dollars . . .

The pencil dropped from his mouth and his hand shot into the air. "One hundred and sixty-two dollars!" he blurted. "The answer is one hundred and sixty-two dollars!"

The other students gaped.

"Th . . . th . . . that's right," stammered Mr. Jupiter, hardly able to believe his ears. "That's absolutely right!"

"It is?" asked Calvin in amazement.

"It certainly is!" exclaimed Mr. Jupiter. "Would you like to try another?

Calvin nodded and put the pencil back in his mouth.

"For the Needy Kitty Cat Food Drive, Ms. Bozzetto collected three hundred twenty cans of Seafood Frenzy," said Mr. Jupiter. "Each cat gets forty cans. How many hungry cats will benefit from Ms. Bozzetto's charity?"

The room fell silent. All eyes watched as Calvin did the calculation.

Just like before, he chewed, chomped, and thought about his notes. He saw himself stacking them into piles of forty . . . two piles, four piles, six piles . . .

"Eight!" cried Calvin. "Eight needy kitties."

"Eureka, he's got it!" shouted Mr. Jupiter, flinging his arms into the air.

"I've got it!" whooped Calvin. "I've got it! I've got it!"

"It's about time," sniffed Stanford.

The next week, during music, Mr. Halfnote organized the class into the four parts of an orchestra. "Woodwinds sit here," he instructed.

Recorders at the ready, Missy, Emberly, and Melvin sat where the music teacher pointed.

"And Melvin," added Mr. Halfnote, "please play your instrument with your *hands* this time."

Melvin nodded.

"Brass is here," continued Mr. Halfnote.

Trumpet in hand, Humphrey took up his position. Ham sat next to him, groaning under the weight of his tuba, while Stanford settled beside him.

"What's that?" asked Ham. He pointed to Stanford's instrument.

"A conch shell," replied Stanford.

"A conch shell?" repeated Humphrey.

In reply, Stanford raised the shell to his lips and blew.

Ba-looooga!

"Nice breath tones," complimented Mr. Halfnote. He pointed to the next section. "Here's where percussion plays."

Jackie made her way toward her chair, carrying her wood block. She was followed by Rose and her triangle, Lenny with his cymbals, Bruce with his glockenspiel, and Calvin with his bongo drums.

"I wonder how many notes we'll earn for this?" Calvin whispered to Bruce.

But Bruce was too busy tuning his instrument to answer.

"Last, but not least, will the string section please take their seats?" said Mr. Halfnote.

Carrying zithers and pushing harps, the rest of the class took up their positions.

Mr. Halfnote rapped his baton on the edge of his music stand for attention.

The fifth graders fell silent. They trained their eyes on their teacher.

There was a suspense-filled pause. Then Mr. Halfnote gave the downbeat, and instantly the orchestra burst into life.

Screeching!

Squawking!

Banging!

Honking!

The woodwinds, brass, percussion, and strings came together in an earsplitting, head-thumping crescendo that filled the room with—

"Music!" said Jackie in a wonder-filled voice. "We're making music." She banged even harder on her wood block.

"Isn't it beautiful?" Ashlee A. whispered to Ashleigh B. Ashlee A. paused in bowing to point out the goose bumps on her arm.

"Ba-looooga," went Stanford's shell joyfully. *"Ba-looooga."*

The music faded.

And Lenny swiped away the tears coursing down his cheeks before anyone saw.

Mr. Halfnote bowed to his students. *"Bravo!"* he cried. *"Bravissimo."*

"Grazie," replied Ham. A look of wonder crossed his face. "Hey, I'm so musically inspired, I'm suddenly speaking Italian!"

"And I'm so inspired, I am going to give each and every one of you ten notes," said the music teacher. He passed out the money.

Calvin stuffed his into his wallet.

But the others barely glanced at their notes. Letting them flutter to the floor, they picked up their instruments once more.

"Can we play again?" asked Humphrey.

"We certainly can!" exclaimed Mr. Halfnote.

"Wait a minute!" cried Calvin, pointing at the abandoned bills. "Are you just going to leave those?"

His classmates nodded.

"Then can *I* have them?"

His classmates nodded again.

Bolting over his bongo drums, Calvin eagerly snatched up the bills. His new and improved math skills told him there must be at least two hundred notes there.

Two hundred!

He couldn't wait to stack them, count them, squirrel them away in his wallet.

He looked around at his poor noteless classmates.

Why did they all look so happy? Didn't they know they were broke?

"Now can we play?" Humphrey begged the music teacher.

"Absolutely," said Mr. Halfnote. Grinning widely, he gave the downbeat.

Grinning just as widely, the fifth graders burst into music again.

Calvin played along. Halfheartedly slapping at his drums, he waited impatiently for the song to end.

The music swirled.

It curled.

It wound its way around the room until finally it found Calvin. Wrapping itself around him, it squeezed tighter and tighter and tighter still, until all he heard was the melody of the song. All he saw were the happy faces of his classmates. All he felt were the bongos beneath his fingers and the joyous thumping of his heart.

I'm making music, he thought with sudden wonder. *Really making music. And—*

He loved, loved, loved it!

More than tetherball.

More than number two pencils.

More, even, than his pile of musical notes.

"Bella! Bella!" whooped Calvin, unable to contain the Italian suddenly surging through him. *"Bellissimo!"*

He banged his bongos with gusto.

* * *

The next morning, the fifth graders arrived to find—

"Doughnuts!" exclaimed Ham. "*Bellissimo* times ten!"

"Who brought the doughnuts?" asked Humphrey.

Calvin stepped forward. "I did." He blushed. "I wanted to do something nice after everyone gave me their notes yesterday."

"But these are *real* doughnuts," said Humphrey. "They had to have been bought with *real* money."

"Yeah, well, I've been saving my allowance like I was saving my notes," said Calvin.

"Was?" repeated Humphrey.

"Was," said Calvin.

Mr. Jupiter winked playfully. "Can you calculate how many weeks' worth of allowance you had to save to pay for these doughnuts?"

Calvin grinned. "Six," he answered, "but who's counting?"

Mr. Jupiter grinned too.

"Hold on a minute!" cried Humphrey. "What did you end up doing with all your notes? Did you finally change your mind about that calculator?"

"Who needs a calculator?" replied Calvin. "No, I found a better use for them." He pointed at the guinea pigs' cage.

Inside, the class pets were cuddled up in a cozy blanket of shredded treble clefs, breath notes, and Mr. Halfnote's face.

"Comfy," said Humphrey.

Then Calvin cried, "Let's eat, and then . . ." He pulled out a set of bongo drums. "Anyone care for some music?"

MORAL: The true value of money is not in its possession, but in its use.

SUNNY DAY

AFTER MR. JUPITER REFUSED TO LET them roast wieners over their Bunsen burners during science, the fifth graders stomped out into the cold February air for recess. They huddled together in a grumbling mass.

"All Mr. Jupiter thinks about is schoolwork, schoolwork, schoolwork," said Jackie.

"'Alphabetize these Latin verbs,'" muttered Rose.

"'Memorize the periodic table of elements,'" groused Missy.

"'Pasteurize your milk,'" added Ham.

Rose nodded. "That was *one* involved science lesson."

Missy shrugged. "It got easier after we caught the cows."

The students fell silent, remembering.

"I bet other fifth graders aren't forced to work so hard," Jackie went on. "I bet other fifth graders are allowed to roast wieners over their Bunsen burners."

The others murmured in agreement.

And Lil waxed poetic:

> *"I wonder as I wander*
> *Across the playground lawn,*
> *What delight might school be like*
> *With Mr. Jupiter gone?"*

The next morning, Mr. Jupiter could not come to class. Overnight he had developed a rash, a sore throat, a ringing in his ears, and smelly feet.

"Scarlet macaw fever," he explained to Mrs. Struggles when he called to report his absence, "probably caught during last weekend's trek across the Osa Peninsula . . . well . . . except for the smelly feet. I get those from my mother's side of the family."

"You poor thing," sympathized the principal.

"Yes, stinky feet are a burden," agreed Mr. Jupiter. "But have no fear, it's just a touch of the bug. I should be back in the classroom tomorrow."

"But what about today?" cried the principal.

"I can't today, although I wish I could," said Mr. Jupiter. "I really don't like leaving my class in the hands of a substitute."

Substitute?

Mrs. Struggles hastily said goodbye, then whipped out her substitute teacher list. She started dialing.

"Oh . . . um . . . uh . . . I'm . . . uh . . . busy today. . . . I'm . . . uh . . . uh . . . shampooing my . . . uh . . . uh . . . horse," stammered the first sub on the list.

"I'm sorry, but I'm allergic," fibbed the second sub.

"Allergic to what?" asked Mrs. Struggles.

"To all things fifth grade," replied the second sub.

The third sub didn't even bother with an excuse. As soon as he heard the words *fifth grade*, he hung up.

"What will I do?" wailed Mrs. Struggles. She flipped to the end of the list and read the last name. Beside it, the former principal had made a notation. It read, "Use only in emergency."

Was this an emergency?

Mrs. Struggles pictured the fifth graders alone in their classroom.

"Ye gods!" she shrieked. Crossing her fingers, she dialed.

By the time the fifth graders filed into the classroom, their substitute teacher was waiting. Her braided hair was covered with sparkly barrettes shaped like bunnies, ponies, and kittens. On her right thumb she wore a purple plastic butterfly ring. And with every step, her light-up tennis shoes flashed a brilliant pink.

"Good glorious morning, my bright-faced chickie-wickies," she chirped. "Oooh, aren't you all sooooo cute!" She swept Emberly into a hug.

"Who are you?" he demanded between twists and wiggles. "And what have you done with Mr. Jupiter?"

The substitute released Emberly and giggled. "Mr. Jupie-Wupie is playing hooky today, so I'm filling in for him. Isn't that fun?" She scrawled her name on the blackboard. "That's me, Miss Day." Over the *i* she put a smiley face instead of a dot, then beamed at the class. "But you can call me by my first name if you like—Sunny."

"Sunny?" repeated Humphrey.

"Sunny *Day*?" snickered Lenny.

"That's my name. Don't wear it out." Miss Day giggled.

"Hey," cried Bruce, "that's *my* line!"

Lenny patted him on the shoulder. "Don't worry about it, buddy. It's just as lame no matter who says it."

They headed to their seats just as Missy shrieked, "My desk! I've lost my desk."

"Get serious," snorted Stanford. "You can't lose a desk."

"But I did," wailed Missy. "Yesterday it was here and today it's gone." She swiped at her eyes. "I lost everything."

Miss Day giggled again. "You didn't lose your desk, silly-willy. I moved it. As a matter of fact, I moved *all* the desks. I thought it would be fun to mix things up a bit."

Missy took a deep, shuddering breath. "Mr. Jupiter never moves *anything*," she explained. "He knows I have trouble keeping track of things, so—"

"So? So? Sew buttons on your underwear!" interrupted Miss Day. "Mr. Jupie-Wupie isn't here. I am. And today I want to have some fun." She hopped up and down and clapped her hands. "Oooh, oooh, I know. Let's play a game. First chickie-wickie to find his desk wins. Ready? On your mark . . . get set . . . GO!"

The fifth graders just stood there, stunned.

Then Ham pointed. "There's my desk, over there behind the Hibernian ceremonial canoe. I'd recognize that choco-roach smudge anywhere."

"You win!" cried Miss Day. Grabbing Ham's hand, she dragged him around the room in a victory lap.

"Stop!" panted Ham. He clutched his side. "Slow down!"

"Wait a second," grumbled Jackie. "That wasn't a fair game. You didn't explain the rules. You didn't give everyone a fair chance. Mr. Jupiter always gives everyone a fair chance."

Miss Day dropped Ham's hand and stuck out her tongue. "Stop being such a party pooper!" she cried. Then she clapped and hopped up and down. "Ooh, ooh, we need a prize. What fun is a game without a prize?" She pawed around in her Pretty Pretty Princess backpack a moment, then beamed at Ham. "Come forward and receive your prize."

"Prize?" said Ham, momentarily suspicious. Then he remembered Mr. Jupiter's prizes. "What is it? Is it a handful of jelly beans? Mr. Jupiter sometimes has jelly beans."

"Oh, it's nothing as boring as that," giggled Miss Day. She dug around in her bag again and pulled out a tube of . . .

"Lip gloss!" she exclaimed. "You win a slightly used tube of Poodle's Breath Pink lip gloss. Isn't that fun?"

Ham shook his head and backed away.

"That particular color will go great with your complexion," said Lenny.

"And your purse," quipped Miss Day.

"Hey, she stole my line *again*!" cried Bruce.

Lenny shook his head. "Mr. Jupiter would never give a prize like that," he said.

Victoria raised her hand. "Miss Day," she said with a flip of her hair. "If Ham doesn't want his prize, can I have it? Poodle's Breath Pink *is* the perfect shade for *my* strawberries-and-cream complexion."

Miss Day squinted at Victoria. "Strawberries-and-cream?" she giggled. "I'd call it tad-yellow-and-smidge-green."

"Hey," bellowed Lenny, "I'm the smart-aleck around here."

"Apparently, I'm just a little smarter and aleckier," joked Miss Day.

"She did it again!" hollered Bruce. "This substitute is a thief—a punch line thief."

"And a know-nothing when it comes to makeup," huffed Victoria.

Miss Day slapped her hands over her ears. "I can't heeear you," she sang out.

The children stared.

And Miss Day grinned. "That's better," she said. She held up their American history textbook. "Mr. Jupie-Wupie wants me to review chapter eighty-six, then introduce fractions, give an organic geochemistry quiz, and go over the steps of the Polynesian commona-wanna-boogie dance, but . . ." She smiled so widely, her back teeth showed. "I thought it would be more fun for me—and you—to have a free day."

"Free day?" repeated Humphrey. "Free day?"

Miss Day suddenly squawked like a parrot. "Polly want a cracker?" She burst into laughter. "Free day. Free day."

"Now she's stealing *my* lines," grumbled Lenny.

"Now, time for more fun!" cried Miss Day. She skipped around the room and up and down the aisles, her tennis shoes blinking. "So, class, what else do you want to do today? Should we put on this suit of armor and joust with brooms? How's about we build a racetrack out of all these old bones and fossils and have guinea pig races? Or maybe . . ." She picked up the skull on Mr. Jupiter's desk. "Bowling!"

"Noooo!" cried the children.

"Well, aren't you all just a bunch of old fuddy-duddies," said Miss Day. "What do *you* want to do?"

"Let's learn about American history," suggested Lenny. He gulped. Had he really said that?

"And wasn't there supposed to be an organic geo-chemistry quiz?" added Melvin. Shocked by the words coming out of his mouth, he clapped his foot over it.

Miss Day crossed her arms across her chest. "But none of that is any fun," she pouted.

"It would be if Mr. Jupiter was here," said Jackie.

At that moment the door flew open.

"Good morning, children," said Mr. Jupiter. He strode to the front of the room wearing an overcoat over his footie pajamas. In his arms he carried a gro-cery bag.

"We thought you were sick!" exclaimed Lil.

"I did feel a bit under the weather earlier," ex-plained Mr. Jupiter, "but I'm much improved now." He turned to Miss Day. "Have they behaved themselves?"

"To tell you the truth, they're kind of dull," replied Miss Day. "All they wanted to do was study history and take science quizzes."

"Science quizzes?" repeated Mr. Jupiter.

"Science quizzes," said Miss Day.

"Polly want a cracker?" squawked Lenny.

The class burst into laughter.

Lenny and Bruce high-fived. "We're back!" they whooped.

"And I'm off," said Miss Day. "Farewell, plucky duckies." Picking up her backpack, she skipped out the door.

Mr. Jupiter turned to his class. "You've all been working so hard that I thought you deserved a surprise."

"A surprise?" repeated Humphrey. "What is it?"

Mr. Jupiter reached into his grocery bag and pulled out a package of hot dogs. "Fifth graders," he said with a grin, "fire up your Bunsen burners."

MORAL: Things are never as bad as they seem.

THE CASE OF THE FUGITIVE FELINE

ON THE TUESDAY AFTERNOON BEFORE spring break, there was a knock on the classroom door and Ms. Bozzetto entered, pulling her art cart behind her. Up until this year, art had always had its own room. But overcrowding had forced the school to add a second kindergarten, so art had become mobile.

"Not unlike the nomadic Xiongnu tribe of the Gobi desert," Mr. Jupiter had said when he'd heard about the change. "Wonderful people, the Xiongnu."

Now Mr. Jupiter clapped his hands to get everyone's attention. "Time for art," he said. "*P-u-t* away your spelling books, please."

"Hey!" said Amisha.

As the students cleared their desks, Ms. Bozzetto reached into the bottom shelf of her cart and pulled out several large reproductions of famous paintings.

"Today," she said, "we are going to discuss the role of the cat in art history."

She held up the first print. "This is a painting by

Mr. Pierre-Auguste Renoir called 'Sleeping Girl with a Cat.' Notice the intense blue of the cat's fur, and how much cuter it is than the sleeping girl."

She held up the next print. "Here is 'Geraniums and Cats,'" also by Mr. Renoir. Aren't those tiger-striped kittens adorable? Obviously, Mr. Renoir adored cats as much as I do."

She held up the last print. "And here is one of my all-time favorites. It's called 'Kitten on a Clothesline,' by Mrs. Sylvia Renoir."

"Was that Pierre-Auguste's wife?" asked Ashlee A.

"No, that's my landlady," replied Ms. Bozzetto. "But art is art, no matter who creates it."

Ms. Bozzetto stowed the prints, then reached into the middle shelf of her cart. She pulled out a purple velvet pillow with gold fringe . . .

"Lovely," commented Victoria.

. . . and a fluffy white cat with green eyes.

"Yeeeks!" chirped the guinea pigs from their cage. They poked themselves, wiggling, between the bars, sniffing and staring.

In Ms. Bozzetto's hands, the cat hung limp as cooked spaghetti.

"Is that a *live* cat?" asked Emberly.

In reply, the cat blinked. Then it lolled onto the purple pillow, which Ms. Bozzetto had placed on top of her art cart, yawned so widely the students could see down its pink throat, and closed its eyes.

"Just a little catnap," snickered Lenny.

In answer, the cat snored, "*ZZZZZZ.*"

Ms. Bozzetto wiped away a string of drool forming under the cat's chin. "Did you know that cats sleep seventeen hours a day? But Mr. Pickles is a particularly heavy sleeper. That's why I chose him for today's art project."

"Today's art project?" repeated Humphrey.

Ms. Bozzetto nodded. "Like the Renoirs, we are going to paint the feline form in all its adorable, sinuous, furry detail. Mr. Pickles will be our model." Reaching into her cart again, she pulled out a stack of paper, some brushes, and several bottles of blue tempera paint. "And like Mr. Renoir, we will be working in this lovely ultramarine blue."

She passed out the supplies.

"Rats," grumbled Rose, having accidentally smeared blue paint on her skirt. The stain blended in with that morning's glue-stick smudge and chocolate-pudding print.

"Now then, boys and girls," instructed Ms. Bozzetto. "I want you to look very closely at Mr. Pickles."

Emberly whipped out his magnifying glass.

Ms. Bozzetto continued. "All objects have shape, or form. Try visualizing Mr. Pickles's form by peeling away all the details and leaving only his framework, or skeletal structure."

"That's one way to skin a cat," quipped Lenny. He looked at Bruce for a response.

Nothing.

"Cat got your tongue?" asked Lenny.

Bruce grinned.

For the next thirty minutes, the students filled their papers with blue tails, blue paws, and blue whiskers.

Mr. Pickles continued to snore and drool and twitch in his sleep.

The guinea pigs kept watching.

Then Ms. Bozzetto clapped her hands. "We've only a few minutes left, so let's begin finishing up," she said.

But the fifth graders never got a chance to finish. At that moment, the school bell began clanging hysterically.

"Fire alarm," Mr. Jupiter said calmly from the back table, where he'd been grading the students' macroeconomics papers. He stood. "You know the drill."

Just as they had practiced dozens of times before, the fifth graders lined up quickly.

Ms. Bozzetto hurriedly checked to make sure the windows were closed, wiping blue paint on her smock as she went.

Mr. Jupiter picked up the guinea pig cage and flipped off the lights. Then he led the students and the art teacher down the hallway and out the nearest exit.

The fifth graders burst out the door and onto the blacktop.

Theatrically, Lenny and Bruce fell into each other's arms, gasping and panting.

"We're alive!" Lenny fake-wheezed.

"Fresh air!" Bruce fake-coughed. He pounded on his chest.

"Knock it off, you two," said Mr. Jupiter. "Fire drills are serious business." He began counting heads. "Is everyone here?"

Rachel shook her head. "Pffft. Pffft."

"What'd you say?" asked Ham.

"Pfcat," repeated Rachel. "Pfcat."

"Did you say 'cat'?" asked Ham.

"Cat!" shrieked Ms. Bozzetto. "We forgot Mr. Pickles!" She lunged toward the school.

But Mr. Jupiter restrained her. "Katrina, you know you can't go back inside. That's a violation of the fire code."

Ms. Bozzetto slumped, then nodded.

"Besides," added Mr. Jupiter, "it's just a drill. Mr. Pickles is completely safe. Mark my words, we're going to return to class to find him peacefully dreaming on his pillow."

But when the students were finally allowed back into their classroom, they found Mr. Pickles—

"Missing!" wailed Ms. Bozzetto. She pressed the now catless pillow to her heart, mixing white cat hair with the smears of ultramarine blue.

"She may be even messier than I am," Rose said to Missy. Then—"Oops!"—Rose stepped backward into the guinea pig cage, which Mr. Jupiter had just returned to the table. Guinea pig fur mingled with her pudding.

Still clinging to her pillow, the art teacher cried, "Oh, where, oh, where has my precious pussycat gone?"

Emberly whipped out his magnifying glass. "This is a case for Emberly Everclass," he declared.

"Get serious," snorted Stanford. "What do you know about detecting?"

"Plenty," replied Emberly. He added proudly, "I've read all six hundred and thirty-six McFardy Boys books, mysteries featuring Marty and Arty McFardy and their bull terrier, Beans."

"Whew," whistled Ham. "I'm impressed."

"I am too," said Mr. Jupiter, "and as much as I want to encourage the discussion of books, Ms. Bozzetto needs our help."

The boys nodded.

"We will organize ourselves into two search parties, just like the time Colonel Wesley Wimberly-Kemp's hot-air balloon was lost in the wilds of Patagonia and I—"

"Focus, Mr. Jupiter," Ms. Bozzetto said.

"Of course," said Mr. Jupiter. "Boys will come with me. Girls will go with Ms. Bozzetto."

"But that's not how it's done," argued Emberly. "This is a mystery. You don't just go searching willy-nilly when you're investigating a mystery. You're supposed to follow clues. You're supposed to use your powers of deductive reasoning. You're supposed to look through a magnifying glass."

"I appreciate your enthusiasm for the detectival arts, Emberly, but Mr. Pickles has gotten a head start." Mr. Jupiter turned to the students. "Class, spread out."

Emberly hung back. That was what the McFardy boys always did when investigating a mystery. They hung back so they could look for clues . . . alone.

Once his classmates were gone, Emberly began searching—slowly, methodically, and with his magnifying glass pressed to his eye. On the door frame, he uncovered a drip of blue paint. In the hall, on Rose's locker, he found a faint blue smudge. And then—

"Aha!"

Outside Nurse Betadine's office, he found half a blue paw print.

"The scoundrel is afoot," he muttered.

Emberly rocked back on his heels and jiggled the coins in his pocket, just the way Arty McFardy always did when *he* was using his powers of deduction. Finally, Emberly said, "I deduce that Mr. Pickles went *that* way."

He walked into Nurse Betadine's office.

"Are you feeling sick?" she asked.

"No, I'm a sleuth," he replied. "I'm solving the Case of the . . . ah . . . the . . . um . . ." Emberly snapped his fingers. "The Case of the Fugitive Feline."

Nurse Betadine shrugged. "Sorry, there's no cat here."

"Mind if I take a look around?" asked Emberly.

"Be my guest," replied the nurse. "But don't touch anything. I just disinfected the place."

Slowly, methodically, and with his magnifying glass pressed to his eye, Emberly searched for yet more clues—on top of the eye chart, inside the Band-Aid box, under the cot.

"Aha!" he cried. "A hairball."

"Impossible," said the nurse. "I keep my office scrupulously clean."

"Impossible indeed," replied Emberly, "and yet there's the evidence. It means Mr. Pickles *was* here. But where is he now? Hmmm?" The boy detective rocked back on his heels and jiggled the coins in his pocket again. Finally, he said, "I deduce that Mr. Pickles, in a fit of gagging, left the comfort of his pillow to seek medical attention here in your office. Unfortunately, you were outside because of the fire drill. Alone, Mr. Pickles gacked up his hairball, and then . . ."

"Yes?" said the nurse. "And then?"

"Then, feeling better, he headed . . ." Emberly walked back into the hallway. Slowly, methodically, and with his eye pressed to his magnifying glass, he searched for clues. He discovered a single white hair lying in front of the gym's double doors. "In here," he concluded.

"But why?" asked Nurse Betadine, following along.

"We're about to find out," said Emberly.

Mrs. Gluteal was washing the sports equipment when they entered. "There's nothing worse than a filthy kickball," she said, looking up from her sudsy bucket.

"Stop!" cried Emberly. "You may be destroying evidence."

"Evidence of what?" asked Mrs. Gluteal.

"Of Mr. Pickles," he said.

"Who?" she said.

"The cat," he said.

"We're on a case," put in Nurse Betadine.

"The Case of the Fugitive Feline," said Emberly.

Mrs. Gluteal rolled her eyes. "Cats would never

come in here," she said. "They don't like all the kick-
ing, the screaming, the hurtling balls." She dropped a
cricket bat into the bucket.

"I know it appears improbable, but we must let the
evidence decide," replied Emberly.

Slowly, methodically, and with his magnifying glass
pressed to his eye, he searched for even more clues. He
searched through a basket of volleyballs and behind
the bowling pins.

"Aha!" cried Emberly. "A mouse toy."

"I've never seen that before in my life," Mrs.
Gluteal said defensively. "I swear."

Emberly picked up the toy. "It's still wet with
drool," he said.

"How unsanitary!" said Nurse Betadine.

Emberly nodded. "Mr. Pickles was definitely here."

"How do you know it was Mr. Pickles?" asked Mrs.
Gluteal. "That toy could belong to any cat."

"It's elementary," replied Emberly, holding the cat
toy with just two fingers. "When I last saw Mr. Pickles,
he was drooling like a Saint Bernard. Only a hyper-
salivating cat could leave a toy *this* wet."

Once again, Emberly rocked back on his heels and
jiggled the coins in his pocket. "I deduce that after

gacking up the hairball, Mr. Pickles suddenly felt frisky, so he came into the empty gym to play." Emberly rubbed his chin. "But then why leave?"

Emberly walked to the door and looked at the room directly across the hall.

"I think I know," he concluded. "Follow me."

He and Nurse Betadine hurried into the school kitchen.

"You'll never believe what happened!" cried Cook when she saw them. "While I was outside for the fire drill, someone ate—"

Emberly finished her sentence. "The tuna-waffle casserole left over from lunch."

"How did you know?" gasped Cook.

Emberly tapped his head. "Powers of deduction."

"Ah," said Cook.

"Obviously, playing in the gym made Mr. Pickles hungry, so he came in here for a bite of lunch."

Nurse Betadine looked around. "But where is he now?"

"Kindergarten room A," said Emberly confidently.

"K room A?" both women exclaimed.

"But why?" asked Nurse Betadine.

"I'd rather not say," said Emberly.

Both women followed him to the kindergarten room. Seventeen little faces looked up from circle time.

"Can we help you?" chirped Miss Fairchild.

"I just want to check your sandbox," said Emberly.

"Certainly," replied Miss Fairchild. She turned back to her students.

Slowly, methodically, and with his magnifying glass pressed to his eye, Emberly pushed aside the plastic molds and shovels until he found the very clue he'd been searching for. "Just as I suspected," he said, pointing. "Mr. Pickles was definitely here."

"Is that what I think it is?" asked Cook.

Emberly nodded.

Nurse Betadine blanched, then shouted, "This sandbox is quarantined. Absolutely no one is allowed to play in it until the sand has been replaced."

Miss Fairchild sighed and looked at a little boy in a dinosaur shirt. "Oh, Aidan, not again."

"It wasn't me," protested Aidan. "Really! It wasn't me."

Emberly rocked back on his heels and jiggled the coins in his pocket yet again.

He wiggled the clues around in his mind, trying to fit all the pieces together. Mr. Pickles had coughed up a hairball, played with his mouse, eaten a bellyful of tuna, and used the litter . . . uh . . . sandbox. What else was there for a cat to do? He thought back to what Ms. Bozzetto had said earlier: *Mr. Pickles is a particularly heavy sleeper.* In his mind's eye he saw the hair-covered pillow.

"Eureka!" exclaimed Emberly. "My powers of deductive reasoning tell me there's only one logical place for him to go. All evidence points to it."

Dashing from the kindergarten room, he raced down the hall, pushed his way into the fifth-grade classroom, and—

Skittered to a dead stop.

"What the . . . !" gasped Emberly.

At the same moment, the others slumped into the classroom.

"That cat's long gone."

"We couldn't find him."

"Poor Ms. Bozzetto. No more Mr. Pickles."

That was when they saw Emberly standing stock-still and clutching his magnifying glass.

"Emberly, what is it?" asked Mr. Jupiter. "You look as if you've seen a ghost."

Struck speechless, Emberly pointed to the guinea pig cage.

Everyone looked.

"I don't believe it!"

"How can it be?"

Inside the guinea pig cage, squeezed between the exercise wheel and a bowl of sunflower seeds, the cat slept peacefully.

"You found my Mr. Pickles!" squealed Ms. Bozzetto.

Mr. Jupiter clapped Emberly on the back. "An excellent bit of detectival investigation, Emberly," he said. "Congratulations."

Emberly blushed modestly.

"Yeah," said Lenny. "But how did Mr. Pickles get in *there*?"

"And what are *they* doing?" asked Rose, pointing to the guinea pigs.

Just outside the cage, the guinea pigs lolled happily on the purple pillow. "Eeek, eeek, eeek," they trilled.

"I believe they're singing a song from the musical *Cats*," replied Mr. Jupiter.

Stanford turned to Emberly. "You may have solved the mystery of Mr. Pickles's disappearance," he said.

"But tell me, supersleuth, how do you explain the whole guinea pig–cat mix-up?"

Slowly, methodically, and with his magnifying glass pressed to his eye, Emberly searched for clues. After a few moments' investigation, he shrugged and scratched his head.

"Impossible," he deduced. "Improbable. My powers of deductive reasoning tell me this is completely illogical."

The guinea pigs smiled up at him.

MORAL: Many of life's mysteries remain unexplained.

ALL TANGLED UP IN MISS TURNER'S CHARMS

MR. JUPITER LOVED SATURDAYS.
Sometimes he went away for the weekend—kayaking in the Bermuda Triangle or attending a scientific conference like the one held the previous week at the Windpassing Institute for Exotic Gases. But on most weekends, he liked to stay home and relax.

One sunny Saturday in April, he rose late, puttered about with his trilobite collection, played a few tunes on his didgeridoo, then sauntered downtown to the Taste of Greece for a bite of lunch. But as he stepped from the restaurant—a trace of stuffed fig leaves still lingering on his lips—he bumped into Miss Turner.

"Paige!" he exclaimed. "I didn't expect to see you this afternoon. What a marvelous surprise!"

Miss Turner grinned. "I was just at the jeweler's having the pachycephalosaurus molar you brought me from your dinosaur dig added to my charm bracelet." She held out her hand so Mr. Jupiter could see. "Isn't it lovely?"

"Almost as lovely as you," he replied gallantly. And

bending low at the waist, he kissed her hand with a flourish. *SMOOCH!*

In a heartbeat, the straps of Mr. Jupiter's pith helmet tangled in Miss Turner's charms.

"Harry," said Miss Turner after a few moments. "You can let go now."

"No, Paige, I can't," he replied. "I'm stuck."

"Stuck?" she cried. She yanked her hand away.

Oomph—Mr. Jupiter came along with it—smash—into the full book bag slung over the librarian's shoulder.

"And people wonder why I persist in wearing this helmet," muttered Mr. Jupiter.

Miss Turner didn't hear him. In an effort to get free, she pushed against Mr. Jupiter's shoulder.

"Easy does it, Paige," he croaked as the straps under his chin tightened. He fell to his knees.

She shoved at his pith-helmeted forehead.

"No . . . no . . . ack!" gagged Mr. Jupiter.

She braced her knee against his chest and—

"STOP!"

Miss Turner lowered her knee. "Sorry, Harry."

Down the block at Bubba's Yarn Barn, Ernest

Moomaday looked out the front window and rubbed his eyes. "I don't believe it," he gasped.

Neither did Rose Clutterdorf. She stood open-mouthed on the corner. "I'm flabbergasted," she said, using one of last week's vocabulary words.

"Paige," begged Mr. Jupiter, who was now a bit breathless from being bent over so long. "Please, please unlatch your bracelet."

"Of course! How silly of me!" exclaimed Miss Turner. She slapped her forehead, or at least tried to.

Oomph—smash!

"Sorry, Harry," she said again. Awkwardly, with her free hand, she fumbled with the clasp, but—

"It seems to be stuck," she said.

"Jeweler," said Mr. Jupiter, whose face was turning blotchy from all the blood running to his head. "Jeweler."

"It's just a few doors down," said Miss Turner. "This way." Carefully, she inched forward a few steps.

Still bowing before her, Mr. Jupiter took a few careful steps backward.

Miss Turner inched forward.

Mr. Jupiter inched backward.

Miss Turner giggled.

"What's so funny?" panted Mr. Jupiter.

"It's like we're dancing!" the librarian exclaimed giddily. And she hummed, "Step-one, step-two . . ."

Mr. Jupiter was feeling a bit light-headed himself. "Have you ever done the cha-cha-cha?" he asked. "I learned it during the season I appeared on *Dancing with the Sort-of-Celebrities*. Watch." And with a wiggle of his hips, he counted off, "One-two-cha-cha-cha."

Miss Turner picked up the Latin beat. "Three-four-cha-cha-cha."

"You're a fleet-footed dancer, Paige," said Mr. Jupiter.

"You should see my tango," she replied.

He laughed. "I'm looking forward to it."

Then, wiggling and giggling, they cha-cha-chaed their way down the sidewalk and into the jewelry shop.

In the Yarn Barn, Ernest said, "I can't wait to tell the guys about this."

On the corner, Rose said, "I can't wait to tell the girls about this."

And they both shivered with anticipation.

* * *

On Monday morning, before the bell rang, Ernest raced to where the fifth-grade boys had gathered on the tetherball court.

"Guys, you'll never guess what I saw this weekend!" he cried.

"A zebra wearing a mink?" asked Lenny.

"Ze mink wearing ze bra?" asked Bruce.

Ernest shook his head. "Mr. Jupiter and Miss Turner, and they were"—he lowered his voice—"wrestling."

"Wrestling?" repeated Humphrey. "Like arm wrestling?"

Ernest shook his head again. "Like *wrestling* wrestling," he whispered.

He waved the boys closer, then glanced around to make sure no teachers were within earshot. "Miss Turner had Mr. Jupiter in a chin lock and wouldn't let go."

"Get serious," snorted Stanford. "There's no such thing as a chin lock."

"There is too," argued Ernest, "and Miss Turner can do one. I saw it with my own eyes."

Lenny spoke up. "I believe it. Miss Turner's a

librarian, and librarians know lots of stuff that other people don't."

"It's all that book reading," added Lenny.

The others nodded.

"Then what happened?" asked Emberly.

Ernest lowered his voice again. "She pushed him, and shoved him, and kneed him in the chest."

"No!" gasped the boys.

"Yes," insisted Ernest. "And the whole time poor Mr. Jupiter's head is snapping up and down and right and left. It was brutal."

Stanford snorted again. "Get serious. Miss Turner is too small to push Mr. Jupiter around."

"She did it, though," argued Ernest. "I saw it."

Lenny spoke up again. "I believe it. Miss Turner may be small, but she's strong."

"It's all that book toting," added Bruce.

"Then what happened?" asked Emberly.

Ernest waved the boys closer still. In the center of their huddle, he whispered, "Mr. Jupiter must have gotten dizzy from being knocked around so much, because he started to walk all wiggly and funny—like one of those guy contestants on *Dancing with the Sort-of-Celebrities*."

"That's embarrassing," said Calvin. "Being beaten up by a librarian and dancing in public."

The others shuddered.

"Then what happened?" asked Emberly.

Ernest paused for effect before saying in an ominous voice, "She dragged him into the jewelry store."

"And?" prodded Emberly.

"And I bought four skeins of recycled-silk yarn and went home," said Ernest.

"What?" cried Emberly. "You mean you didn't shadow them? You didn't tail them? You didn't do any sleuthing?"

"I had to be home by two," said Ernest.

"Argh!" wailed Emberly in frustration.

"One doesn't need to be a sleuth to figure out what happened," said Stanford with a sniff of superiority. "It's obvious that Miss Turner bullied Mr. Jupiter into buying her some jewelry."

Ham spoke up. "Poor Mr. Jupiter."

The others nodded in agreement.

"Maybe we should send him an encouragement card," Ham went on. "My mom always sends me encouragement cards whenever bad stuff happens. One time, I ate too many chocolate crullers and threw up and I got a card that read: 'Things will get better, I have a hunch, even though you lost your lunch.'"

Lenny snickered. "Yeah, our card could read: 'Unlike Ham, you didn't hurl. Instead, you got beaten up by a girl.'"

"Get serious," snorted Stanford. "Mr. Jupiter's been through enough humiliation. He's been degraded, discountenanced, and mortified. Do we really want to add to his discomfiture?"

"Huh?" said Ham.

"Quit using next week's vocabulary words and speak English," grumbled Calvin.

Stanford translated. "I don't think we should let on that we know. The guy's already been embarrassed enough. Why make it worse?"

The boys considered Stanford's words.

Then Calvin said, "The brainiac is right. Let's zip our lips and throw away the keys."

Melvin pretended to do just that—with his toes.

At about the same time the boys were talking, Rose waved to the fifth-grade girls hanging around on the monkey bars.

"Yoo-hoo, ladies," called Rose. "Have I got juicy news for you."

The phrase *juicy news* worked just like a magnet. Unable to resist its pull, the girls gathered around Rose.

"Start at the beginning," insisted Bernadette, flipping open her investigative reporter's notebook. "And tell all."

"Well," began Rose, "on Saturday morning I woke up early, ate a bowl of Toastie Oaties, and dressed. But when I went to look for my shoes, the left one was missing, so I limped around the house looking under cushions and—"

"Hold it," said Bernadette. "What's so juicy about a missing shoe?"

"Nothing, unless you find it full of apple juice or something," replied Rose. "But you told me to start at the beginning, so—"

"Just tell the juicy parts," interrupted Bernadette. "I don't care about your stinky shoe."

Added Lil poetically:

> *"Rosy, dear Rosy, spill out the*
> *scandalous,*

But please delete how you limped around
sandal-less."

"Oh, okay," said Rose. "So I was standing on the corner of Olympia Avenue and Delphi Street when I noticed Mr. Jupiter and Miss Turner in front of the Taste of Greece. At first they were just talking and acting normal. Then all of a sudden, Mr. Jupiter grabbed her hand and . . ." Rose paused again.

"And?" urged Bernadette.

"And"—Rose's eyes twinkled—"he kissed it."

"Oooh," squealed Ashlee A. and Ashleigh B. in unison. "How romantic." They swooned into each other's arms.

"Is there anything more?" asked Bernadette. She prepared to close her notebook.

"Uh-huh," said Rose.

"Well?" urged Bernadette.

"Well, Mr. Jupiter wouldn't take his lips off her hand," continued Rose. "She tried to get him to stop. She struggled to pull away, but he held on tight. And the whole time he was holding on, he was begging her to do something."

"Do what?" asked Bernadette.

Rose shrugged. "I was too far away to hear, but I can guess."

Ashlee A. and Ashleigh B. looked at each other and cried in unison, "Will you marry me?" They swooned into each other's arms again.

"Do you think it's true?" gasped Bernadette. "Do you think Mr. Jupiter proposed?"

Rose nodded, a knowing smile spreading across her face.

"Why? What do you know?" persisted Bernadette.

"I know that Mr. Jupiter got down on his knees and begged some more. That's when Miss Turner stopped struggling. Then together they went to . . ." Rose paused a moment, then announced triumphantly, ". . . the jewelry store."

The girls fell silent as the words sank in. Then they exploded in an ear-shattering chorus of oohs and aahs, squeals and whoops and hollers.

Lil waxed poetic:

> *"My love is like a red, red rose,*
> *That's newly sprung in June,*
> *My love is like a melody,*
> *That's sweetly played in tune."*

And Jackie pretended to talk into a microphone. "There you have it, sports fans. Round one of the love match between the teacher and the librarian. Some say it's going to be the love story of the century. Others say it's going to be a storybook wedding. Either way, it's love."

"Do you think we'll be invited to the wedding?" Ashlee A. asked.

"I can't wait to congratulate the bride and groom," said Ashleigh B.

"Hold up," said Bernadette, closing her notebook. "I don't think we should let on that we know. I mean, this is sort of a personal event. Maybe we should wait until they tell us."

The others considered Bernadette's words.

Then Rachel spoke up. "Pffft."

"She's right," said Lil. "Our lips are sealed."

"Sealed with a kiss," added Rose.

The bell rang. The fifth graders—boys and girls alike—filed into their classroom.

Mr. Jupiter met them at the door. "Good morning, class," he said. "Did you have a nice weekend?"

"Oh, yes," answered Bernadette. "It was *love*-ly."

All the girls smiled widely.

Lenny said, "Hey, Bruce, how do you think Mr. Jupiter's weekend went?"

Bruce shrugged. "*Beats* me."

All the boys blushed and lowered their eyes.

Mr. Jupiter studied his students a moment. "Perhaps," he finally said, "I should tell you what happened to *me* this weekend."

"Oh, yes!" begged the girls.

"Oh, no," groaned the boys.

MORAL: Every story has two sides.

FABLES FROM THE FIFTH

MR. JUPITER ASKED THE FIFTH GRADERS
to take out their writing journals.

"Today we are going to create our own fables," he
said.

"Fables?" repeated Humphrey.

Mr. Jupiter nodded. "As you know, a fable is a short
story that teaches a lesson."

"Blech," gagged Lenny. "I hate . . ."

Mr. Jupiter raised his eyebrows.

"I mean . . . I . . . um . . . uh . . ."

"Detest?" suggested Stanford. "Despise? Abhor?"

"Yeah, that's it," said Lenny. "I *abhor* stories that
teach lessons. Who wants to read a sappy tale about
sharing, or telling the truth, or recycling your old
sneakers?"

"Not me," said Bruce with a shudder.

"Fables *do* teach lessons," said Mr. Jupiter, "but
they are also meant to be entertaining. As a matter
of fact, fables often use talking animals or magical

objects to make their point." He looked around the room. "Does anyone remember what the point in a fable is called?"

No one answered.

"The moral," Mr. Jupiter informed them.

"I abhor morals," said Lenny.

"Ah, but in a fable the moral often pokes fun at foolish deeds," said Mr. Jupiter.

"Pokes fun?" repeated Humphrey. "I'm all ears."

Mr. Jupiter opened a copy of *Aesop's Fables*. He read aloud the story titled "The Tortoise and the Hare."

"So," he said when he had finished, "what do you think?"

The students looked at each other in confusion.

Then Bernadette said, "I don't get it."

"Yeah," said Jackie, frowning. "I don't understand why the fast guy didn't win. I know for a fact that the fast guy *always* wins."

"What a lame-o story," opined Emberly.

Mr. Jupiter sighed. "Let's try another one." He read "The Boy Who Cried Wolf."

"I don't believe it," declared Melvin when Mr. Jupiter had finished. "What kind of goofy writer lets his main character get eaten by wolves, then leaves out all the good, gory details?"

"That's right," agreed Calvin. "You're always telling us that good writers use good details."

"Boy, that Aesop sure was lousy," added Ham.

"Boooo!" cried Ashlee A. and Ashleigh B. in unison. "Boooo! Hissss!"

Stanford gave a superior sniff. "I could write a better fable than that."

"I'm glad you think so," said Mr. Jupiter, "because that's exactly what you all are going to do. Using your own experiences, I want each of you to ask yourself what advice you would give to your fellow classmates. Use that advice as the moral for your original fable. Are there any questions?"

No one raised a hand.

"Then begin," said Mr. Jupiter.

For the next half hour the room was silent as the fifth graders followed the four steps of writing— prewriting, drafting, revising, and editing.

Then Calvin slapped down his tooth-marked pencil. "Done!" he cried.

The others put down their pencils too.

Mr. Jupiter looked around the room. "Would

anyone like to share his or her fable? Ham, what did you come up with?"

Ham stood, smoothed his paper, and read:

The Camels and the Cookie

A long, long time ago, two camels went to a Chinese restaurant. They ordered wonton soup, egg rolls, beef chop suey, war mein noodles, crab rangoon, crispy jumbo shrimp with garlic and scallion sauce, and the pu pu platter for two.

"Mmmm," said the first camel, "pu pu."

Finally, the waitress brought fortune cookies.

The second camel grabbed his cookie and snarfed down the whole thing. All of a sudden, his face turned red, his eyes popped out of his skull, and he fell on the floor. Then he started clawing his throat and making choking sounds. In about a minute he was dead.

The first camel ate the leftover pu pu all by himself.

MORAL: Take out the fortune before you eat the cookie.

The class clapped and whistled.

"That was much better than Aesop," said Ernest.

Victoria flipped her hair. "Wait until you hear *my* fable."

Standing, she read:

The Sheep and the Fashion Police

Once upon a time there was a really, really super-white sheep that pranced around all summer long.

Prance. Prance. Prance.

She had the whitest wool in the whole flock.

Prance. Prance. Prance.

Her white coat was so bright it hurt the other sheeps' eyes.

Prance. Prance. Prance.

Then one day it wasn't summer anymore. It was fall. But the really, really super-white sheep kept prancing around.

The fashion police arrested her and put her in handcuffs.

"What did I do?" asked the really, really super-white sheep.

*"You broke a fashion law," said the police.
"You wore your white coat in the fall."
They dragged her off to jail.*

MORAL: Never wear white after Labor Day.

The class clapped and whistled and stamped their feet.

Jackie looked down at her clothes. "Does that rule apply to socks and underwear?"

"You want to know about socks and underwear?" cried Lenny. "Have I got a fable for you."

The Armadillo and the Accident

Once there was an armadillo who always went around wearing messy clothes.

"I like this story already," said Rose.

"Shhhh," shushed the others.

Lenny continued:

His pants were all raggy and his shirts were all holey. "Who cares how I'm dressed?" the armadillo asked.

"I do!" exclaimed Victoria.

"Shhhh!" the class shushed again.

Lenny went on:

> *One day the armadillo stepped onto the highway and—*
>
> *Splat!*
>
> *A semitruck ran him over.*
>
> *His blood oozed all over the road, and his guts were hanging out, but he wasn't dead.*

"Yes!" cried Melvin.

"Shhhh!"

Lenny concluded:

> *The armadillo was rushed to the hospital, where the nurses and doctors ripped off his shirt and pants to fix his wounds. But guess what? His underwear was as yucky as the rest of his clothes. And he had to lie there on the emergency room table in dirty, holey underwear in front of everybody. And he died, not because he got run over by a truck, but because he was totally embarrassed.*

MORAL: Always wear clean underwear in case you get in an accident.

The fifth graders leaped to their feet. They clapped, whistled, stamped, and pumped their fists in the air.

"That fable was fantastic-o!" opined Emberly.

"It was," agreed Ashlee A. and Ashleigh B. "It really was." And they cheered:

> *"Hey, you, Aesop, get out of our way,*
> *'Cause fifth-grade fable writers are here*
>   *to stay.*
> *We're better—uh-huh!*
> *We're better—uh-huh!*
> *We're better—*

"Hooray!" the whole class shouted.

Mr. Jupiter sighed.

MORAL: People often cheer an imitation and hiss the real thing.

CR-E-P-U-S-C-U-L-E

IT WAS THE FIRST SATURDAY IN MAY, and sweaty-palmed contestants from eleven schools— along with their beaming parents, bored siblings, cheering friends, and hopeful teachers, as well as the superintendent, who had to be there because it was her job—crammed Aesop Elementary School's auditorium for the district-wide spelling bee.

"Are you nervous?" Missy asked Amisha. Along with some of the other fifth graders, Missy had come to cheer Amisha on.

"*N-o,*" replied Amisha. She lifted her chin. "I'm a spelling goddess."

"Maybe," said Ham, "but you have some stiff competition." He pointed to the other contestants lining up onstage. "Isn't that Rex Lexicon, the third-grade whiz kid from Petronius?"

"Yeah," said Jackie, "and there's Dorcas Wordsworth, aka the Great Wordini. She's won this competition two years in a row."

"Don't forget about little Mikey Mapes," added Calvin. "He may be only five years old, but he's a genius. I hear he's going to Harvard next year."

"Oh, *p-l-e-a-s-e*," drawled Amisha. "Not one of them can hold a candle to my orthographic brilliance."

"Huh?" said Ham.

"Her good spelling," translated Stanford.

"Oh," said Ham. "I get it." He thought a moment. "But can you spell it?"

"*O-r-t-h-o-g-r-a-p-h-i-c   b-r-i-l-l-i-a-n-c-e*," speed-spelled Amisha.

Ham whistled. "I'm impressed."

"If you've got it, flaunt it," Amisha said smugly.

"Well said!" exclaimed Victoria.

"It's true," continued Amisha. "I'm better than anyone else on that stage." She puffed out her chest. "Do you think Rex Lexicon can spell *crepuscule*? I can."

She stuck her nose into the air.

"Do you think Dorcas Wordsworth knows the language of origin for the word *flibbertigibbet*? I do."

She plastered a haughty look onto her face.

"Do you think little Mikey Mapes can even reach the microphone?"

Her friends shook their heads.

"Well, I can," declared Amisha.

At that moment, Mr. Jupiter—wearing a long black robe and a powdered wig in honor of his position as a judge—stepped up to the microphone. "All contestants, please report to the stage. All contestants to the stage, please."

"See you in the winner's circle," said Amisha. And with her nose still pointed at the ceiling, she strutted toward certain victory and . . .

. . . straight into Miss Turner's bulging book bag.

Amisha tripped. She stumbled. She careened—off balance and arms flailing—across the stage, knocking over the microphone . . .

SQUEAK!

The audience slapped their hands over their ears.

. . . bumping into the judges' table . . .

THUMP!

Mrs. Struggles snatched at the dictionaries sliding onto the floor.

. . . plowing into little Mikey Mapes . . .

SMASH!

"Mommy!" wailed the five-year-old.

. . . before landing with a loud *THUD!* flat on her face.

In the audience, kids laughed.

Parents looked concerned.

Teachers rushed forward to help.

Stunned and red-faced, Amisha scrambled to her feet.

"Are you all right?" asked Mr. Jupiter. He patted her shoulder. "Is anything bruised?"

Just my pride, thought Amisha.

But she shook her head and stammered, "I'm— I'm . . . fine."

Mr. Jupiter nodded. "Then take your seat, please."

Amisha hobbled over to her chair and took her place between Rex and Dorcas. Waves of humiliation crashed over her, washing away her confidence. She no longer felt like a spelling goddess. She felt like a sweaty-palmed contestant instead.

She turned to Rex. "Are you nervous?"

"M-e?" Rex snorted. "Never."

She turned to Dorcas. "Are *you* nervous?"

"N-o," said Dorcas with a roll of her eyes. *"I'm* the Great Wordini."

Amisha fidgeted in her chair. Beads of sweat broke out on her forehead, and her stomach fluttered faster than Mr. Jupiter's motorized swim fins. To calm herself, she spelled *crepuscule* over and over in her head.

The kid from Marcus Aurelius went first.

"Your word is *nonplussed*," said Mr. Jupiter. "Gus was *nonplussed* by the fuss made by Russ. *Nonplussed*."

The kid didn't hesitate. "*N-o-n-p-l-u-s-s-e-d*," he answered.

"Correct," said Mr. Jupiter.

Smiling, the kid returned to his seat.

Next up was little Mikey Mapes. He climbed onto a stool and leaned into the microphone.

"Please spell *nausea*," said Mr. Jupiter. "Spelling bees can cause *nausea*. *Nausea*."

Mikey thought a moment. "*N-a-u-s-e-a*," he finally answered.

Mr. Jupiter smiled and nodded.

Hopping off his stool, Mikey skipped back to his seat.

Rex was next.

"Watch and learn," he whispered to Amisha before stepping up to the microphone.

"Your word is *doodlesack*," said Mr. Jupiter. "Angus

MacTavish refers to his bagpipes as a *doodlesack*. *Doodlesack*."

Rex puffed out his chest. "*D-o-o-d-l-s-a-c-k,*" he speed-spelled. He shot the judges a smug look.

"No, I'm sorry, that's incorrect," said Mr. Jupiter.

"But . . . but . . . ," began Rex.

"Please step off the stage," said Mr. Jupiter.

Looking like he had been slapped, Rex slumped away.

Dorcas was next.

"Now you'll see how the *great* ones do it," she whispered to Amisha. She approached the microphone.

"Your word is *flocculence,*" said Mr. Jupiter. "*Flocculence* should never be confused with flatulence. *Flocculence*."

"That's soooo easy," drawled Dorcas. "I, the Great Wordini, spell words like that in my sleep."

"Then spell it, please," said Mr. Jupiter.

Dorcas rolled her eyes. "*F-l-a-t-u-l-e-n-c-e*." She smirked at the judges. "See? I told you so. I don't stink."

"I'm sorry," said Mr. Jupiter. "That's incorrect."

"What?" shrieked Dorcas.

"Please step off the stage," said Mr. Jupiter.

"But I'm the Great Wordini!" cried Dorcas. "I always win the spelling bee."

"Not this year," said Mr. Jupiter.

Furious, Dorcas stomped offstage.

It was Amisha's turn.

Gulping, she stepped up to the microphone and faced the judges.

"Your word is *orthographic*," said Mr. Jupiter. "Spelling bee contestants are very *orthographic*. *Orthographic*."

In the audience, Amisha's friends grinned at one another.

"She knows this one," whispered Missy.

"And watch her flaunt it," Victoria whispered back.

But Amisha didn't flaunt it. Standing in the spotlight, her heart pounding and her stomach fluttering, she could barely contain her nervousness. Crossing her legs and bouncing from foot to foot, she slowly, carefully began to spell. "*O-r-t* . . . um . . . um . . . *h-o-g-r* . . . ah . . . ah . . . *a-p-h-i* . . . ummm . . . *c*?"

"That's correct," said Mr. Jupiter.

Relief washed over her.

Mr. Jupiter grinned. "You may return to your seat."

And so the bee went. Word after word. Contestant after contestant.

The speller from Socrates went down in the second round.

But not Amisha.

The speller from Cicero went down in the fourth round.

But not Amisha.

The spellers from Homer, Petronius, and Caesar went down in the seventh round.

But not Amisha.

By the tenth round, only Amisha and little Mikey Mapes remained onstage.

Mikey climbed onto his stool and leaned toward the microphone.

"Your word is *beriberi,*" said Mr. Jupiter. "Strawberries are good, but *beriberi* is bad. *Beriberi.*"

Mikey shot Amisha a triumphant look before spelling, "*b-e-r-r-y-b-e-r-r-y.*"

"No, that's incorrect," said Mr. Jupiter.

"Mommy!" wailed Mikey. He ran offstage.

Mr. Jupiter turned to Amisha. "If you can spell this next word, you will be our new district-wide spelling champion. Are you ready?"

Amisha took a deep, calming breath and nodded.

"Your word is *crepuscule*," said Mr. Jupiter. "*Crepuscule* is a word always used in spelling bees. *Crepuscule*."

Amisha wanted to laugh at the easiness of the word. She wanted to show off by speed-spelling. But then Miss Turner's book bag caught her eye. Slowly, methodically— no flash, no sass—Amisha spelled, "*C-r-e-p-u-s-c-u-l-e*."

"That's correct!" cried Mr. Jupiter. "Amisha Spelwadi, you are the new district-wide spelling champion!"

The audience cheered.

The superintendent presented Amisha with a bee-shaped medal, then posed for a few quick photographs before racing back to her office.

And Amisha's friends crowded onstage to congratulate her.

"You *are* a spelling goddess," squealed Missy. "You really are!"

Amisha blushed. "Naw," she said. "I'm just a fifth grader who can *s-p-e-l-l*."

MORAL: False confidence is the forerunner of misfortune.

ANOTHER HISTORY LESSON

TOWARD THE END OF MAY—AS HE HAD every single Friday morning since the beginning of the school year—Mr. Jupiter said, "Let's begin by reviewing some American history. I trust everyone read last night's assignment?"

As always, Ashlee A. bit her lip.

Ashley Z. tapped his pencil.

Calvin quickly looked at Stanford.

"Stop!" cried Stanford, holding up his hand like a traffic cop. "I didn't read it, okay? I was busy studying something else, so I didn't read it. Geez!"

Mr. Jupiter sighed. "Didn't anyone read their American history last night?"

Lenny's hand shot into the air. "I did!"

"You did?" said Mr. Jupiter. He waited for the punch line.

It never came. Instead, Lenny said, "It's taken me most of the school year, but I've read the *whole* book. And you know what? History isn't half bad."

"It isn't?" said Calvin.

"Actually, it's kind of exciting," continued Lenny.

Mr. Jupiter nodded. "Why don't you tell us what you learned, Leonard."

"Well," said Lenny, "it all began when the British put a tax on stamps. Boy, this made Americans so mad, they wanted to lick them. They were still steaming about that stamp tax when the British took away America's favorite drink. 'Give us liber-tea or give us death!' cried the Americans. Even dogs took to the street in protest, an event we now call the Boston Flea Party."

"Wait a second, Leonard," interrupted Mr. Jupiter.

But Lenny was on a historic roll. "So the leaders of the American colonies—those guys in wigs and three-cornered hats—decided to declare themselves free from England and George the Third's cruel rule."

"Very accurate," complimented Mr. Jupiter.

"Go on," urged Calvin, leaning forward. "What happened next?"

"England didn't want the colonies to be free, so there was a war."

Bruce rubbed his hands together with glee. "I love war stories."

"Get this," confided Lenny. "The whole American Revolution is a war story."

"Who knew?" said Bruce.

"It's all right here," said Mr. Jupiter, tapping the history text.

The fifth graders ignored him.

"Tell the rest," pleaded Calvin.

"So the wigged guys said 'Rats!' to the British and called up George Washington at his house, Mount Vermin, and asked him to lead the American army."

"Mount Vernon," corrected Mr. Jupiter.

Lenny was too absorbed in his story to hear. "George Washington was one fierce army dude, even if he did have hippo teeth. He power-slammed the entire British army—sometimes called Tories—straight into the Atlantic Ocean. He was helped by some Massachusetts Minutemaids."

"I believe you mean minute*men*," said Mr. Jupiter.

"In one famous battle, George Washington crossed the Delaware River," Lenny went on.

"Why did he cross the river?" asked Bruce.

"To get to the other side," answered Lenny.

"Actually," began Mr. Jupiter, "the Battle of Trenton was important because—"

Lenny cut him off. "And you want to hear the weirdest part?"

Heads around the room nodded eagerly.

"Birds—lots and lots of them—took part in the Revolution."

"What?" exclaimed Mr. Jupiter.

"It's true," said Lenny. "I read it on Chickipedia."

Mr. Jupiter waved his hands. "No, no, no!" he cried. "That's completely untrue. How many times have I told you not to trust online sources? Believe me, birds took no part in the Revolution."

"What about Patrick *Hen*-ry, John *Jay*, Benjamin Frank-*loon*?" said Lenny.

Mr. Jupiter looked at him, bewildered.

"So then what happened?" said Calvin.

"The Patriots (that's us) trounced the Redcoats (that's them) in a close war. The Patriots almost lost a couple times, but after a last-minute surge, they beat the Redcoats. The final score was eighty-nine battles to eighty-seven battles."

The fifth graders whooped triumphantly.

And Ashlee A. and Ashleigh B. leaped to their feet.

"Ready?" cheered Ashlee A.

"Okay!" cheered Ashleigh B.

Then, stomping and clapping, they cried:

> *"Don'tcha know?*
> *Can'tcha guess?*
> *Patriots are the very best!*
> *Go back, Redcoats, go back home*
> *And leave our USA alone!*
> *Gooo, Patriots!"*

"I'm thrilled by your enthusiasm," Mr. Jupiter shouted above the cheering, "but I'd like to redirect the lesson to—"

Lenny cut him off again. "Let me teach you a song I learned last night," he told the others. "It's from the Revolution."

Minutes later the students—and guinea pigs—were singing:

> *"I'm a stinky poodle, Randy, stinky*
> *   poodle do or die . . .*
> *Stinky poodle went to town, just to find a*
> *   hydrant . . ."*

Mr. Jupiter shrugged. "They may not have the *full* scope of history yet," he said to himself, "but it's a start. Yes, it's definitely a start."

MORAL: Little by little does the trick.

HAPPY GRADUATION

MAY TURNED TO JUNE, AND AESOP Elementary School buzzed with excitement. Fifth-grade graduation was just a day away, and everyone wanted to celebrate.

In honor of the occasion, Mr. Halfnote composed a special arrangement of "Happy Days Are Here Again" for armpit, washboard, and Burmese spectacled guinea pig.

Cook baked a triple-layer chocolate crawfish cake with the words OH, JOY! piped across the top in red frosting.

And Mrs. Gluteal, along with Mr. Frost and Mrs. Chen, performed a "happy dance" every day in the teachers' lounge for two straight weeks.

"We can't wait . . ." *Tap-tip-tap.*

"For them to graduate." *Tippity-tap-tap-tap-tap.*

"You know," said Miss Turner, "I'm actually going to miss them."

Mrs. Gluteal quit tapping.

"In fact," Miss Turner continued, "I'm going to miss *all* of you."

"What are you talking about, Paige?" asked Ms. Bozzetto.

Miss Turner turned to Mr. Jupiter. "Shall we tell them, Harry?"

He smiled and nodded.

"Harry was told by scientists that chimpanzees can't dance, so he's off to Tanzania to prove them wrong," she said in an excited rush. "And *I'm* going with him. After all, chimps need the Dewey decimal system just as much as they need the rhumba."

"You mean you're leaving Aesop Elementary?" gasped Mr. Frost.

"After tomorrow, my work here is done," explained Mr. Jupiter. "It's time to move on."

"That's right," enthused Miss Turner, pumping her fist in the air. "Full steam ahead!"

For a moment, there was stunned silence as the teachers took in the news.

Then Mr. Halfnote pounded Mr. Jupiter on the back.

Miss Fairchild pecked Miss Turner's cheek.

And Mrs. Gluteal cried, "Brownies for everyone!"

At the far end of the table, Mrs. Shorthand, the

school secretary, whispered into Mrs. Bunz's ear, "After *these* monkeys, teaching chimps should be a breeze."

"I've said it all along," replied Mrs. Bunz, *"weird."*

That afternoon, the fifth graders cleaned out their desks and turned in their textbooks. Already Mr. Jupiter had packed up his smilodon teeth and shrunken heads; his Lungunga pig masks and his owl pellets. He had hauled away his mastodon skeleton, his Byzantine funeral urn, and his Venus flytrap. He had even given the guinea pigs to Mr. Halfnote. "I'm sure the three of you will be very happy together," he had said.

Now teacher and students looked around at the bare walls and empty shelves.

"That's it. The room's clear," Lenny declared. "All that's left to do is graduate."

"Then it's *adiós,* Aesop Elementary, and *hola,* Aristophanes Middle School!" cried Bruce.

The fifth graders cheered and high-fived each other.

"Aren't you excited too, Mr. Jupiter?" asked Rose, noticing his glum expression.

"I think the word *bittersweet* better describes my emotions," replied Mr. Jupiter.

"Huh?" said Ham.

Stanford rolled his eyes. "Bittersweet," he translated, "means bitter and sweet at the same time."

"Like choco-roaches?" said Ham. "Mmm . . . bittersweet."

Mr. Jupiter smiled. "Something like that."

The next morning, Mr. Jupiter and his fifth graders—along with their happy parents and even happier former teachers—assembled in the auditorium.

Proudly, the children took their places onstage.

Mr. Jupiter smiled at Emberly's shirt and tie, Amisha's high-heeled sandals, and Bruce's slicked-down hair. "Don't you all look nice," he said.

"You look nice too," said Rose, who had managed to get to school that morning without smearing strawberry jam on her sleeve.

"Thank you," Mr. Jupiter said, looking down at his brightly colored Akkadian ceremonial tunic. "A special occasion does deserve a special outfit."

"I couldn't agree more," said Victoria as she adjusted her tiara.

Mr. Jupiter turned to the audience. "Parents and teachers," he said, "thank you for attending this very special ceremony in honor of our children's years at Aesop Elementary School."

In her seat, Mrs. Bunz giggled.

"This ceremony, however, is not an ending, but a beginning," continued Mr. Jupiter. "While our fledglings may be flapping away from *this* nest, they are soaring toward bright and glorious futures."

Mrs. Bunz giggled again.

"And so," said Mr. Jupiter, "to commemorate this remarkable occasion, I want to present each of our graduates with a special award—a token, if you will, of my admiration and esteem."

Mr. Jupiter moved to a table covered with papyrus scrolls. "These are made from scraps that I excavated during my last trip to the sacred Temple of Philae." He coughed, trying to clear the lump that was growing in his throat, then added, "I crafted them with my own two hands especially for my students."

Mr. Jupiter looked at Miss Turner. "Paige, will you help me?"

"Certainly, Harry," she said.

Standing behind the table, she handed him the first scroll.

"Hamilton Samitch," Mr. Jupiter called out.

Ham stepped forward.

"Ham, I present you with the Gastronomic

Philosophy Award," said Mr. Jupiter, giving him the scroll.

Ham turned to Stanford.

"The science of good eating," translated Stanford. "You've just received the Science of Good Eating Award."

"Oh," said Ham. "Mmmm."

From the audience, Mr. Samitch shouted, "Can you hold your scroll a bit higher, Hammy?"

FLASH!

"Now can you and Mr. Jupiter shake hands?"

FLASH!

"Cheese," Mrs. Samitch hollered out.

Ham pulled a round of cheddar from his pocket.

FLASH!

Then, glowing with pride and blinking rapidly, Ham groped his way back to his seat.

Miss Turner handed over the next scroll.

"Rachel Piffle," called out Mr. Jupiter.

Rachel stepped forward.

Mr. Jupiter smiled. "Rachel," he said, "I'm pleased to present you with the award for the Most Eloquent Use of Monosyllables."

"Pffft," said Rachel. "Pffft."

She accepted her scroll, then, suddenly and unexpectedly, flung her arms around Mr. Jupiter.

"Pffft," she said again.

And then . . . she whispered, "I'll miss you, Mr. Jupiter."

Breaking away, she rushed back to her seat.

Mr. Jupiter slumped and ran the sleeve of his silk tunic over his eyes.

"Harry," said Miss Turner, "are you able to continue?"

Mr. Jupiter squared his shoulders. "I've faced monsoons, typhoons, and man-eating raccoons," he replied. "I can get through this."

Taking the next scroll, he said in a voice that still cracked a bit, "This year, the Dodecahedron Award for Advanced Mathematical Studies goes to . . ."

Stanford stirred in his chair, preparing to rise.

"Calvin Tallywong," announced Mr. Jupiter.

"Calvin?" cried Stanford.

"Me?" cried Calvin as he made his way across the stage.

"Yes, you," replied Mr. Jupiter as he handed over the scroll. "No one in our class has made more advancements, mathematically speaking, than you have."

"That's my boy!" shouted Mr. Tallywong from the audience.

"Get serious," snorted Mrs. Binet under her breath. "I'll be speaking to the principal about this."

Onstage, Mr. Jupiter was ready to give the next award. "Stanford Binet," he called.

Sulkily, Stanford came forward.

"Stanford," said Mr. Jupiter, "you are indeed a stellar student. But there is one area in which you have truly excelled. That's why I am presenting you with the E.L.T.I.E.P. Award."

The other students looked confused.

"The *what* award?" Ham finally asked.

"The Excellence in Language Translation, Interpretation, Explanation, and Patience Award," translated Stanford excitedly. "Can you believe it? Me? The E.L.T.I.E.P.!"

"That's my boy!" shouted Mrs. Binet from the audience.

"Let me take a picture for you," offered Mr. Samitch. *FLASH! FLASH! FLASH!*

Bruce was next. He received the Rubber Chicken Award for Hijinks and Humor.

Emberly received the Solver of Enigmas, Conundrums, and Cat-astrophes Award.

And Ashlee A. and Ashleigh B. each received an award for Most *Cheer*-full Countenance.

"Rah, rah, sis boom bah!" cheered their families from the crowd.

And so it went. One by one, the almost–sixth graders accepted their awards.

Victoria won the Most Likely to Be Seen Draped in Organdy Award.

"That was obvious," she sniffed.

Humphrey won the Echo Award for Repetition and Redundancy.

"Echo?" he repeated.

And Melvin won the Junior Contortionist Award (with a gift card for a free bag of Twistorelli Pretzels).

He accepted his award with his toes.

Finally, just one student remained.

"Leonard Wittier," called Mr. Jupiter.

Lenny stepped forward and looked up at his teacher.

"Leonard," said Mr. Jupiter, his voice cracking with emotion, "I present this papyrus scroll to"—he took a steadying breath—"to the Most Improved Student."

Lenny took the award. He searched his mind for a snappy comeback, a funny punch line, a clever zinger. But all he could come up with was "Gee . . . thanks."

In her seat, Mrs. Bunz could barely contain her glee. "It's almost over," she squealed. "Any second now."

Onstage, Mr. Jupiter struggled with his emotions. "And now," he finally said, "by the power vested in me as your fifth-grade teacher, I declare that each and every one of you has met the requirements and conditions necessary to graduate from Aesop Elementary School. Therefore, it is my honor to be the first person to call you . . . . *sixth* graders!"

At his words, the auditorium erupted into joyous pandemonium.

The graduates tossed their scrolls into the air.

Their parents leaped from the seats and hugged each other.

And the armpit, washboard, and guinea pig band burst into "Happy Days Are Here Again."

Then the teachers, parents, and band members all streamed into the lunchroom for cake.

Mr. Jupiter hung back. "I'll meet you in there," he said to Miss Turner. "I . . . I . . . just need a moment to compose myself." He ducked into the prop room.

As for the brand-new sixth graders, after picking up their scrolls, they lingered onstage.

"So we did it," said Missy.

"We're graduates," said Rose.

"Sixth graders," said Amisha.

From the lunchroom came the sounds of celebration.

But onstage, all was quiet.

Finally, Ham said, "Bittersweet."

"Uh-huh," sighed Stanford.

And then Lil stepped forward. Raising an imaginary cup, she waxed poetic:

> *"Oh, dear little school, we've learned here*
>   *so long,*
> *But now we must bid you goodbye!*
> *We've filled you with laughter; we've*
>   *trilled you with song,*
> *And occasionally fought, teased, and*
>   *cried.*
> *Thy walls they have witnessed math,*
>   *spelling, and art,*
> *And have echoed with poetic lines.*
> *So, our teacher,*

Our classmates,
Goodbye and boo-hoo,
Farewell, little Aesop,
To you."

Touched by her words, the others all raised imaginary cups too.

Then, after a moment of silence, Bernadette said, "You know what I'll miss most about Aesop Elementary School? Mr. Jupiter."

Victoria suddenly burst into tears. "Me too!" she bawled. "Me too."

Bernadette pulled a tissue out of her purse. "Here," she said, handing it to Victoria, "your mascara is dripping all over your satin."

"Who cares?" wailed Victoria. "Beauty isn't everything."

It was the perfect opportunity—a chance to fling a real zinger. But—

"This is no time for jokes," Lenny said to Bruce.

Bruce nodded seriously.

"We're all going to miss Mr. Jupiter," Calvin spoke up. "But we'll just have to look on the bright side. Now that we've graduated, Mr. Jupiter can finally go back to his former life of big adventure."

"Yeah," agreed Lenny. "Mr. Jupiter's ridden an ostrich across Kenya and floated weightless in orbit. Compared to that, two years with us must have been really, really boring."

"On the contrary," said Mr. Jupiter, stepping out of the prop room.

"Hey," said Calvin, "you heard us talking."

"Every word," admitted Mr. Jupiter. "And I have a few things I'd like to add, if I may." Pulling over a folding chair, he sat down with his former students.

"Adventures," he began, "aren't just about rafting down raging rivers and climbing up rugged mountains. They're also about the people you've been on those adventures with—the Sherpa guides, the witch doctors . . ." He paused, then added, "The students."

The sixth graders looked at each other, pleased.

"Do you mean that teaching *us* has been an adventure?" asked Lenny.

Mr. Jupiter smiled, his eyes shining. "My *greatest* adventure."

"You were *our* greatest adventure too," snuffled Victoria. She blew her nose with a loud, wet honk.

Mr. Jupiter grinned. "That's lovely of you to return the compliment, Victoria, but I'm betting there are lots more extraordinary adventures ahead for each and every one of you."

Both teacher and students reflected on their futures for a moment.

Finally, Mr. Jupiter broke the spell. "I've suddenly got a taste for some cake. Shall we?"

"But first," called out Miss Turner as she made her way down the auditorium aisle toward the stage, "let's take one last class picture." She held up the camera she'd borrowed from Mr. Samitch. "Ready?"

Mr. Jupiter and his students wrapped their arms around each other and looked toward the librarian.

"Everyone say *adventure*!" shouted Lenny.

"Adventure!"

FLASH!

Mr. Jupiter laughed. "Look out, Aristophanes Middle School, here they come!"

MORAL: Do boldly what you do at all.